EVIL IS
ALWAYS
HUMAN

EDDIE WHITLOCK

UNITED WRITERS PRESS
ATLANTA, 2012

EVIL IS ALWAYS HUMAN
EDDIE WHITLOCK

ISBN: 978-1-934216-73-6

First Printed Edition, March 2012

Printed in the U.S.A.

to Mama Cat

*"Evil is unspectacular and always human,
and shares our bed and eats at our table."*

— W. H. Auden —

Chapter I
HANGING

⊰⊱

May 11, 1912

Mama didn't have to holler a second time that morning. We was up and getting ready as soon as we could be. We was going to a hanging, likely the onliest one we would ever see, to hear Daddy tell it. He had been in a good mood for a week or two, talking about it.

"I seen a fellow get hung one time when I was little," he said at supper right after he had heard about this one. "It's a sight. I didn't think they'd do no more of them out where you could see them. They got to where they do them inside and can't nobody see them."

Daddy wanted to go and we did, too. Living on Mr. Caudell's place, working his fields, there weren't much to do but work. Taking a day off and going to see a hanging sounded like a right good time to all of us. I weren't but about twelve years old. If it hadn't been for taking care of Little Carl, I would have been in the field just like Mama and Daddy by then.

"You reckon he's going to let us go?" I asked my sister Gladys right after Daddy talked about the hanging.

"He ain't letting us stay here without him." I knowed she was right.

If Daddy went, we went. Didn't none of us go nowhere without him. He didn't go nowhere without us. It was the way we was. There was many a time that Daddy would need to go do some business with the folks that we worked for. If he had left us at home, we could have got some work done, but he took us with him every time.

It had been that way where we lived before and it was that way now with Mr. Caudell. Even if all Daddy was doing was going down there to tell him that a plow was busted or that we needed fertilizer, we all went.

A hanging, though, was something different. I got to thinking. We hadn't never been to nothing just to have a good time. A hanging was special and we was all getting to go.

Daddy told us that we would leave for it early that morning right after we fed the animals and eat. Mama didn't say nothing about it. She was busy with the baby while Daddy was getting the mules and the wagon ready for our trip to town.

Mama and Gladys was getting things together for us to take. Mama was holding the baby while Gladys filled up a croaker sack with what we was taking. I had finished feeding the chickens—that was my job every morning—and was helping Little Carl get dressed.

Little Carl was my brother. He weren't much younger than me, less than a year, I think, but most of the time he needed help with everything he done. He had got kicked in the head when he was little and never got over it. Sometimes, Little Carl would slip into a spell, which Daddy called his "idiot spell," and he would just set and stare with one eye half-closed and his mouth hung open.

He would go a good while without having a spell. Then he would go another good while having them all the time. There weren't no telling how he would do, especially on a trip like going to the hanging. We didn't go nowhere like this so there just weren't no telling.

It made Mama sad to have to mess with Little Carl so I had took him on to raise, I guess you would say. Since the baby was born, Mama was pretty busy anyhow, so it weren't like she had time for two at once anyhow.

When I got Carl dressed and pulled my boots on, we went outside to the wagon. In a minute Gladys came out, too, toting the baby and the croaker sack. I helped Little Carl up on the back of the wagon and then turned around and helped Gladys. She hung on to that baby, giving me the sack.

Gladys was a little older than me, old enough that if she'd ever had a chance to meet boys, she would have probably had a boyfriend. She was a pretty girl, but a little on the skinny side like the rest of us. She had black hair like the rest of us did except for Daddy. His hair was brownish and bushy and it always looked like it was trying to get off his head it would stick up so.

Us younguns all got on the back of the wagon. It and the mule belonged to Mr. Caudell, just like the house we lived in and the land we worked. I didn't figure Daddy had asked him about using the wagon to take us to the hanging. I knowed that we was allowed to use it for trips we had to make to town and to go to church, though we didn't never do that. It was taking a day off from the farm that Mr. Caudell might not like. Still, it was a hanging and there probably weren't much farming going on that day anywhere in the county. You had to figure the man would expect us to want to go see it.

Mama came out and went to the outhouse. She had done sent each of us there, knowing that the trip to town would not include any pee-stops. When Mama finally came to the wagon, Daddy got the mules going. It would take a good while to get to town and he would be in a bad mood if the trip got slowed down.

As we got going, us younguns slid down to the rear end of the wagon so we could talk low and not have daddy hear us. You didn't want to make him mad, though. He said he wasn't going to put up with us acting up. He never did.

Once we got going good, the noise of the wagon rolling on the road was enough for us to be able to talk some at the back of the wagon, if we was careful.

"Gladys, who they hanging?"

My sister Gladys was a right smart girl. She could figure things out good without knowing everything there was to know. Before the baby was born, she had started doing some of the cooking to help Mama out. She could make most anything worth eating, which was good on account of us not having no whole lot of choice about what we was going to eat.

EVIL IS ALWAYS HUMAN

"It's a man name of Paul Tidwell. I heard Mr. Caudell talking to Daddy about it last week. They was setting on the porch, talking about our bill down at the store. Mr. Caudell mentioned it on account of figuring the store would be closed on Saturday so all the folks what work there could go see it."

"Why they hanging him?"

"He killed his wife and his two little girls right after Christmas," Gladys told us.

Little Carl was listening to her, having a pretty good day that day. "Why did he do that, Gladys?"

The truth is that Gladys didn't know at all why the man killed his wife and them two little girls, but Gladys was good at thinking and she thought up a good story and we didn't much care whether it was true or not, as long as it was good. You just had to catch her in the mood to talk. She weren't always in such a mood. Some days she would be all blowed up like a bullfrog and wouldn't say nothing to nobody but Mama and then it weren't but a word or two.

I was right glad she was in a talking mood that day. "He was crazy," Gladys told us. "He said the devil had got into them."

We didn't go to church, but we knowed who the devil was. The devil was who folks blamed when they done something bad and got caught at it. I didn't much figure it was the devil getting into folks as it was folks just getting caught and wanting to blame somebody else for it. You see that a lot.

"The devil is bad," Little Carl said a bit too loudly. Daddy's head turned a bit, but he didn't speak.

We set there quiet for a bit of time, not wanting Daddy to stop that wagon. It would be bad for us if he did.

"His wife was a big fat woman," Gladys whispered to us, making Little Carl grin and hold his mouth to keep from giggling out loud. "She would've made three of him. The little girls were fat, too. All three of them eat the groceries so bad that Mr. Tidwell had all he could do to try to feed them.

"He was a little bitty man, like I told you. He couldn't hardly see without his glasses."

"I bet he weren't wearing them glasses when he married that fat woman!" Little Carl whispered and we all held our mouths then.

Gladys went on. "He had done got put off of the Upson place," she said. "Mr. Upson accused him of slacking off and letting crops rot in the ground, but he said he was doing his best. Him just having them two girls and no boys to help him made it rough. Between trying to feed them women and trying to make a crop for Mr. Upson, little Tidwell weren't getting much of neither one done. He got into it with Mr. Upson and he got put off. He took a place on the McKillips' property for a while, but then he got on with the Tate Brothers."

Everybody knowed the Tate Brothers, Peter and Paul. Folks called them "Pete and Re-pete" because the older one had been a jack-leg preacher until he saved up enough money to buy some farmland. Peter Tate liked to talk about Jesus this and the Good Lord that and his little brother Paul would Amen! every comment. They was the kind of fellows that didn't have nothing to do with you lessen they could make a dollar off of you. There was a lot of them kind of folks.

Most landlords didn't much care about the eternal souls of the folks that worked for them. The Tate Brothers did. All landlords let their folks — even the colored hands — off to go to church on Sunday morning. The Tate Brothers made their tenants go to church. If you didn't go, they would run you off.

Tidwell had never been a religious man. He went to camp meetings and to revivals, but everybody done that. When the Tate Brothers told him he would be expected at services as part of his arrangement, he didn't argue. It sounded to him like he was getting a Sunday morning break.

More like, it would be a chance for the Tates to talk poor Tidwell into donating to them any little piddling profit they didn't take some other way.

"Mr. Tidwell went to Peter Tate's church, the Temple of Apostolic Faith," Gladys said. We knew of the place because it was the only brick building on our end of the county. "They had a new, young preacher name of Kelly and he was really drawing crowds with his preaching. Peter Tate had hand-picked the Kelly fellow because he was single and wouldn't need much of a salary to minister the place. This fellow made folks feel bad about how they was and good about how Jesus was and folks that go to church regular really like that."

I didn't say anything to that. I knowed that Gladys had to be laying it on then because she wouldn't know about why this fellow had been the preacher. We had been to church three times. One time was after Little Carl got kicked. It was long and hot and I about went to sleep except they would sing and wake everybody up. I reckon if you run a church, you know you got to do something to keep folks from sleeping through the whole thing.

The other times we had been was for funerals. The first funeral was for my granddaddy, a man I didn't never meet. He was Mama's daddy and it was the only time I know of that we seen any of Mama's people except for Aunt Clara. They all come over and spoke to Mama. Daddy didn't say nothing to none of them and they didn't say nothing to him.

Gladys went on with her story. "Mr. Tidwell got to liking church more than anybody would have ever expected him to. Some folks is like that. They get to hearing how good Jesus is and the next thing you know they want to be just like Him, make Him proud of them in a way most folks tries to make their mamas proud. The preacher give him a old Bible and told him to read it and he did. He read it cover to cover, only he couldn't read that good and he missed a good bit of it. Most folks don't bother reading the whole thing. They just go for the parts somebody told them was good. Mr. Tidwell was trying to make something of it, I reckon.

"Something started happening when cotton come in, though. The Tate Brothers were expecting more to make than did." The end of summer had been dry and the bolls didn't fill out like they should have. Daddy had been lucky that the patch he farmed was a little better than Tidwell's. It had still been a rough year for all of us, just especially rough on Mr. Tidwell.

"Mr. Tidwell asked the preacher for help and, of course, the preacher told him to give his troubles over to the Lord. That's what preachers do when you got troubles. They tell you to let God handle them for you. Mr. Tidwell went to praying, begging the Lord to improve the cotton, to make them bolls fill out nice and pretty, to give him a miracle like He had done for so many others, to hear the preacher tell it.

"Didn't nothing come of it, no matter what Mr. Tidwell done nor how much he prayed nor nothing. The Lord didn't hear Mr. Tidwell's prayers no more than He hears yours or mine. No, Mr. Tidwell had a year so bad that the Tate Brothers were of a mind to put him off the property. It was that preacher Kelly that talked them into letting the man stay on another year.

"Mr. Tidwell, he didn't know why the Good Lord didn't see fit to give him a miracle like he done for Moses and for Noah and for the people at the wedding what had run out of wine. If the Good Lord could give wine to drunkards, why couldn't He give cotton to a poor man trying to keep his head above water?

"Mr. Tidwell got to thinking that he didn't get his miracle because the Lord didn't find him worthy of it. He kept looking at hisself, his life, everything, but he couldn't find nothing that he thought God would hold against him. He weren't sinning. There weren't nothing he could be sinning about. He didn't have much of nothing and he was giving more than he could to the church on Sunday, but he still weren't getting no word back on his praying.

"He tried setting a bush on fire one day, on account of that being how God had talked to folks sometimes, but all that done was start a fire in the little garden he had going behind his house. It liked to have burned up everything he had growed and still he didn't hear God say nothing. Preacher Kelly told him you can't push God to talk, that God talks when He wants to. The preacher said you hear God the best when you read His Word. Mr. Tidwell went back to it full-force.

"He was setting at home one day, reading his Bible and his wife asked him why he was doing that instead of re-planting collards in their little garden that had burnt up.

"I believe that's when he figured it was Mrs. Tidwell and the girls. It weren't him falling short in the eyes of the Lord. It was them. He would see them, whispering and talking while he was praying. He got to where he would pray with one eye shut and the other one looking at them. He got to thinking more and more about that, about how that woman and them two little girls was living in the ways of the world while he was trying his best to live in the ways of the Lord."

Little Carl was listening with his mouth hung open. He weren't having one of his idiot spells, I don't reckon. He was just listening, but he sure looked funny doing it. The baby was sleeping, laying in Gladys's lap wrapped up tight in a blanket like a Indian papoose. Mama would do that to keep the baby warm. I wondered why it was sleeping so good. The road was rough and the mules didn't seem to miss a single rut or rock as we went.

Gladys was quiet for a couple of minutes. I was scared that Little Carl might come to hisself and holler for her to go on, but he didn't. Gladys was staring at the baby and I wondered if she was seeing something that I wasn't. I never heard her talking to it much, but I figured she loved it. I just wished that she would tell it because I thought that would make it feel better, but she was just looking at it, not saying nothing.

I looked up at Mama and Daddy. They was setting on the seat, looking straight ahead, not paying a bit of attention to one another or us either. Mama was wearing a dress that was a pale brown with little red flowers all over it. She had a sweater on over it. She was wearing her boots, but she had cleaned them off good and oiled them with grease and they looked right nice. Daddy was wearing a clean shirt with his overalls. Mama didn't get many chances to wear a dress. Mostly she wore work clothes like the rest of us. We was wearing the clothes Daddy had got for us back at the first of the year. Lots of younguns didn't wear shoes, but we did. Gladys had stepped on a nail one time and her foot swole up and like to have busted open. After that, Mama made us all wear boots when we was outside. Daddy cussed her over it, but she didn't pay him no attention on that one.

We rode on.

When Gladys started talking again, she had dropped her voice. She sounded like she did when she got worked up about something. She would get all serious and breathing hard. She hadn't done that much since the baby was born. "Mr. Tidwell wondered why his wife and girls weren't praying with him.

"He had heard about the devil getting into folks and he was pretty sure that was what had happened to his wife and to his little girls. They was in cahoots with the devil and they was working against him."

Little Carl, who acted like he was listening and thinking the story through, whispered, "So he killed them!"

My sister shook her head and her straight black hair fell across her face. "Not right then," Gladys told Little Carl. "He was sure he could pray the bad out of them."

"He couldn't though!" Little Carl said a little too loud. Daddy's head turned just a little bit and I was afraid we were about to catch it. He didn't say anything, though. We waited a little while before Little Carl poked Gladys and nodded for her to continue.

"No, he couldn't, but he sure did try. He went to talk to that young Preacher Kelly about it, to try to find out what he needed to do about his women and the devil that had got into them. When Mr. Tidwell got to the church, he found out that the new young preacher was gone.

"It turned out he had met a girl in town and wanted to marry her. He had asked Paul Tate for a raise. The church had twiced as many folks coming as it had done before and it was taking in a good bit more money. Paul Tate didn't much care for the young preacher no how. He said he was too flashy with his slicked-down hair and pretty lips and green eyes. The Tate brothers got to talking about Kelly and how he was acting. Peter Tate decided that he could run the church hisself until they could get another preacher hired. Turn-out was always good around Christmas, so the offering would be right hefty, too. They had put Kelly out, told him to leave the place they let him live in and get on. Didn't nobody see Kelly after that.

"So there weren't anybody at the church when Mr. Tidwell got there. He stepped inside that big stone building, hollered and didn't hear nothing but the echo. The whole place sounded hollow, empty, like even the Lord God had up and left town. Mr. Tidwell walked up the aisle, looking up at the empty wood cross they had hung up at the front. There had been a picture of Jesus on the wall by the side door, but Preacher Kelly had took it with him when he left. It was like the devil and come and got Mrs. Tidwell and the girls and now he had even got Jesus and the preacher.

"If the devil had took the preacher, then he could take anybody, use anybody. Mr. Tidwell went home, expecting that he might very well run into the devil hisself when he got there. The first one he saw was Becky, the older girl, setting on the steps outside the front door. She was eating a glass of cornbread and buttermilk. She was so busy eating that she didn't hear her daddy walk right up to her.

"She looked up, her little pig nose wiggling up and down, the buttermilk running down the left corner of her mouth.

"He come walking up on her setting there and he weren't thinking about her being his little girl. He was thinking about the devil and whatever mischief the devil had put into her. He looked at her and said, 'You got the devil in you!'

"She took another bite of buttermilk and cornbread and said, 'No, I ain't.' Mr. Tidwell got mad then because he thought the devil was poking fun at him. He run up the steps and grabbed Becky by the hair and drug her into the house with him. She was hollering and her mama come running out of the back room. Mr. Tidwell looked at his wife and said, 'You got the devil in you.'"

"She looked at him and I reckon she knowed that he was going crazy if he hadn't done gone. She tried to say something to him, but he slapped her in the mouth. 'You got the devil in you and you got these girls working against me.' She was a big old woman, but he slapped her a second time hard enough to drop her to the floor.

"Before she could get up, he drug Becky into the bedroom and throwed her on the bed. 'You got the devil in you!' he kept hollering at her. Becky was trying to get aloose from him, but he was hitting her every time she would try to raise up.

"Mrs. Tidwell finally got up and she come running in there behind him and grabbed ahold of him and pulled him off the little girl. He turned around and pushed her and she went backwards into the wood stove and hit her head against it and died right there. They found her with the side of her face busted open and her head caved in. Her eyes was still open, though, and it was like she was looking over at where her head was messed up, looking to see what had killed her.

"Becky had got up off the bed and was trying to get to the door. Mr. Tidwell took her by the neck and squeezed so hard that she couldn't breathe. She was pulling at his hands, moving her lips to beg him to stop, but he weren't hearing none of it.

Little Carl was so intent on Gladys that I was scared of what was going to happen when the story was over. If he got too excited and went to talking loud, Daddy would stop the wagon and that wouldn't be good for any of us. I couldn't help but wonder if Little Carl was thinking of when he got kicked in the head. I didn't know whether he remembered that happening or not.

Gladys kept going. "He choked her till she quit struggling. When she quit struggling, he stood up and went back across the front room to the back room to see if the other little girl, Ruth, was in there.

"He didn't find her. He came back out and found Becky trying to crawl to the front door. He went over to the stove and got a poker and come back and hit her in the head with it. He took the poker and shoved the sharp end into her back and pushed it through her.

"She was still trying to crawl when Ruth came around to the porch from the outhouse. She screamed when she saw Becky and her daddy. She thought somebody else must have hurt her sister and that her daddy was trying to take the poker out of her.

"Little Ruth went running up to them, screaming as she ran. She got right up to her daddy before she seen it in his eyes."

"Seen what?" Little Carl hollered.

Daddy stopped the wagon and we hushed and looked at him and then down at the floorboards. He turned around in the seat and pointed at us. "What the hell is going on back there?" he hollered.

We didn't move. He didn't get out of the seat. If he had been going to whip us, he'd have gotten up as soon as he stopped. Even so, he would come up out of that seat in a heartbeat if we spoke or dared to look him in the eye. I looked down, studied my boots. Little Carl was retarded, but he done the same thing.

"I ain't going to stop again, am I?" he asked us.

"No, sir," I said. Little Carl echoed a few seconds later.

"If I stop again, there's gonna be ass-whippings all around. You understand me?"

"Yes, sir." Pause. "Yes, sir."

"I ain't took a day off from that farm for nigh on three years. I'll be god-damned if I am going to let you mess it up."

We didn't say anything because he hadn't really asked us anything. I looked up then, though, and saw that he was staring right at Gladys. And Mama was staring right at him. I looked down. If you looked Daddy in the face when he was mad, he thought you was getting smart with him and he didn't care for that. He'd whip you good for getting smart.

The baby rustled a little and I was so afraid that it was going to cry, but it didn't. Daddy turned back around and whistled and the mules started again.

Gladys didn't say nothing. All three of us knowed how lucky we were. I was glad Daddy wanted to go to this hanging so bad. Otherwise, he would have tore us up. It would have been bad except for that hanging.

When the wagon started rolling along again, we didn't say anything to each other. I thought we might ride the rest of the way like that, but I sure hoped not. Gladys and her story was making the trip a heap more interesting. We were going by a cemetery and there was one grave toward the road that was pretty fresh. The dirt was still red and piled on top and hadn't packed down yet. It looked like a baby's grave from the size of it.

I looked over and seen that Gladys was looking at the baby she was holding and wasn't paying any attention to the cemetery. She took her finger and wet it in her mouth and then stuck it in the baby's mouth and it took to sucking on it. I wondered if it was getting bigger. I knowed it ought to be, but it didn't look no different than it had at first. It was a mighty little thing.

Little Carl was looking at the cemetery and I knowed it was probably going to stick with him that he had been hearing that story about Mr. Tidwell killing his little girl and here we was, driving by a baby's grave. If we had ever knowed any of the folks that lived around there, we might have been able to figure out whose baby that was, but we didn't. It weren't nothing that mattered. I just wondered whether them folks had other younguns besides that one. It seemed like it made it better if there was other younguns besides the one that died. I really didn't know. It just seemed that way to me on account of there being three of us.

I looked up at Daddy, but I was careful doing it. If I met his eyes, that would be all she wrote. I didn't though. He was driving the mules and not paying no attention to me at all. I was sure proud of that. Mama's head was still cocked a little to the side, like she might very well be watching him on the sly, watching to see if he was going to blow up at us.

Gladys started talking again. She didn't drop her voice real low. I thought it was because she was in the middle of that story for us and couldn't help herself. "Little Ruth is the one that lived long enough to tell the sheriff who had done it. She weren't but six years old and Mr. Tidwell was a full grown man. He drug her back in the house to the bed and he went at it.

"When the Sheriff found her, they said her bottom half was tore in two. She was still alive, crying and saying, 'Daddy, Daddy, Daddy' over and over again."

I didn't know whether Little Carl understood what Gladys had said. He was back to setting there, looking at our big sister and not seeming to have a thought in his head except her and what she was saying.

"Then what happened?" he whispered so soft if I hadn't known what he was going to say, I wouldn't have known.

"Mr. Tidwell walked all the way to Macon. He made it all the way there, too.

"Paul Tate come out to their place that evening. He brung a bag of oranges and nuts for the younguns of all the tenant farmers. It was something that Peter Tate didn't abide. He called giving anything to somebody that didn't earn it 'coddling.' Peter Tate said that it was in the Bible that coddling folks was a sin because it made them lazy."

"Mr. Caudell don't bring us nothing for Christmas," Little Carl said softly. "I reckon he don't take to coddling neither."

That was for dern sure, I thought to myself. Mr. Caudell didn't have nothing to do with nobody but the men of the families that worked his places. I remembered one time him coming to the house to talk to Daddy. Mama was setting on the porch with Little Carl. The little fellow was still getting over the head-kick. She kept a bandage on his head because that one spot kept draining and needed to be covered up.

She was trying to get Little Carl to look at her when Mr. Caudell come up. He didn't say a word to her, walked right on by and opened the door to the house. He went in and looked around, come back out and started toward the back. He hollered for Daddy, not even bothering to ask Mama where he was at. I remembered watching him, watching him act like we weren't there at all, just walking by us.

Gladys had come out the door with a bowl of mashed up beans for Mama to try and feed to Little Carl. It was about the only thing he eat for a while there. Gladys looked at Mr. Caudell and if he looked at her, he didn't let on, but he had to have looked at her when he went through the house, looking for Daddy.

Mama told us later that a man like Mr. Caudell didn't trust hisself around women. That was why he didn't even speak to her. I didn't understand what she was talking about, but Gladys told me later. Gladys said that she'd heard Mr. Caudell had a high yellow baby on account of his nature. I didn't find out what that meant for a good while and I was mighty ashamed when I did.

"No," Gladys said, "Mr. Caudell ain't like that, I don't reckon. But Mr. Paul Tate sees hisself as a Christian man and tries to live up to it every now and then. When he brought that bag of oranges and nuts, Mr. Paul saw the door was standing open and walked up. He seen Becky laying there, the poker still stuck through her. It about scared him to death, coming up on that little dead girl like he did. She was laying there, twisted around with blood and pee oozing out of her.

"Mr. Paul stumbled backwards down the steps and run back to his wagon and high-tailed it to town. He got the marshal out there as soon as he could.

"The marshal went in and got to looking at Becky. Then he heard a moan from the next room and found Ruth, about bled to death. She kept saying 'Daddy, Daddy, Daddy,' while they tried to pick her up, but then she sort of just fell open and that's when the blood started coming up into her mouth, like it didn't have anywhere else to go. The marshal never told nobody but his wife what that little girl said."

"She said, 'Daddy, Daddy, Daddy,'" Little Carl offered softly.

"No," Gladys said so low that I had to lean forward to hear. "No, she said, 'Devil, Devil, Devil.'"

Now of course that weren't the end of the story nor no way to end a story. It was just where Gladys decided to stop. Little Carl was staring off into the woods that we was driving past. The baby was starting to twitch some. It was looking around and acting like it might up and holler. I hoped Gladys would be able to take care of it before it done anything to make Daddy mad.

I don't know how much longer we rode. I must have dozed off. I woke up with my head laying in Little Carl's lap, him looking off into the woods. We was coming into town and I set up to try and focus my eyes on what was going on. There was a lot of folks on the road, lots of buggies, people walking, all of them laughing and having a good time.

All of them folks had come to have a good time, to see a hanging. It was might early for so many folks to be about for foolishness like that, but folks didn't get to have a good time too often, so I reckon they was all out to make the most of it. One little man and his fat wife walked by us and I thought about Mr. Tidwell. I thought about him killing his wife and Becky and Ruth. I knew that Gladys had probably made up the story, but still, it was as true as whatever might have been told in court.

Daddy was having a idiot spell hisself, you might say. He was driving them mules along right slow with his mouth hung open and him looking all around at the crowd of people that was there. "I bet there's a thousand people here," he said really low and shook his head. I think that was the first time I ever seen him look like that. He was grinning. I hadn't never seen him grin except when he was mad about something and was getting ready to whip somebody. That was how he done.

Daddy put the wagon in the alley behind the post office where some other folks had already parked. The baby had woke up and Gladys sat for a while feeding it while the rest of us just set there without saying nothing. When it finished, she burped it and we started down. I carried our croaker sack and we followed Daddy out of the alley and onto the street.

Daddy walked ahead of us. I held Little Carl's hand and the

croaker sack and tried to keep up. I won't lie to you. That many folks at one time scared me. Trying to walk through the crowd made it hard to keep up. Mama was behind us, shoving us along and Gladys was behind her.

We turned the corner onto what they called Washington Street that run in front of the courthouse. The jail was a part of the courthouse and the gallows was a permanent part of it. There was a heavy wood-beam rack that was right outside the jail on the second floor of the courthouse. I reckon they put the jail up there to keep the prisoners from trying to escape, but it looked to me like it just give them a better view if they was to look out the window.

It was a better view as long as you didn't look toward the rack, now that I think about it. I reckon it wouldn't be that good a view if you might be swinging from a rope sometime soon.

Daddy stopped, looking up at it, so we stopped, too. A deputy come out and walked around, looking down at the crowd while he kept his hand on the pistol that he toted. Several folks hollered up to him, calling him by name and he would wave down to them, but he never did smile and he never did take his hand off that pistol.

I wondered if he thought there might be trouble, what with there being that many people. I wanted to tell him we had all come to see the hanging, that he didn't need to worry about trouble unless somebody decided not to hang Mr. Tidwell. I kept my mouth shut, though, because I was still a youngun and you sure didn't tell grown folks nothing when you was a youngun back in them days, especially not grown folks with pistols.

"When's the hanging?" Daddy hollered up to the deputy.

"Twelve," he said. "You got about a hour."

Daddy nodded to the man up on the scaffold and kept walking. People had already spread blankets on the area all around the gallows. We walked a ways before Daddy saw a rise ahead and went to it. Even though we were a good ways back, we had a good view and even if anybody sat in front of us, we'd be able to see over them.

Mama spread the quilt she had brought out on the ground and set down on it. Gladys handed her the baby and then she set down next to Mama. It was funny how the women folks could set down and be still when the men — me and Little Carl and Daddy — couldn't. Daddy stood there beside us for a minute then his feet got to itching and he walked over to where some men was standing and talking by the Confederate Memorial.

That memorial was the tallest thing in town besides the courthouse. It was a tall skinny thing with a statue of a soldier up at the top. The soldier was a rebel wearing a fancy suit like he was in charge, not the little cap a lot of fellows wore that they had got from their granddaddies. The statue soldier was facing north, they said, so that he could be on watch for the Yankees that had whipped us fifty years before.

The men standing around must have all knowed each other. They didn't seem to have nothing to say to Daddy when he walked up. I seen him go over there, seen him talk, but we was too far away to hear anything being said. Besides that, folks was talking all around, talking about the hanging, about the weather, about Jesus and about what they would have for supper when they got home. Talking.

Daddy didn't hang around that bunch too long. They didn't seem to take to him so he walked over and stood next to two old men wearing Confederate uniforms and setting in chairs with wheels on them over in the shade next to the courthouse barn. I could see Daddy talking up a storm to them, but to be honest with you, they didn't look like they could hear a word he was saying.

Me and Little Carl had ants in our pants and Mama finally told us to go see if there was some other younguns we might could play with. We took off.

Sure enough, there was some boys about our ages standing around a pile of bricks and two saw horses across the street from the courthouse. Me and Little Carl went to them. There were five or six of them and one of them asked us where we was from.

"We live on Mr. Caudell's property," I told him and then I told him our names.

Little Carl was just standing there, his mouth hung open.

"What's the matter with your brother?" a boy named Russell asked me.

"He ain't right."

"He's got a messed-up side of the head, ain't he?" Russell said.

"Yeah," I told them. "He got kicked."

The boys examined Little Carl's head, looking at the white scar and the rumple in his forehead on the lefthand side. Little Carl didn't much know how to act around other younguns and — to be honest — I don't reckon I did neither. We had been around cousins a couple of times, but that was it and that had been before we got big enough to be away from Mama and Daddy.

Little Carl started coming to hisself and said, "Daddy let us come see the hanging because he was afraid there might not never be another that they let folks see."

"Ain't nothing wrong with him when he talks," one of the boys said. "I figured he was a jew baby."

"No," I told them. "He ain't no jew baby. Little Carl talks pretty good when he's in his right mind. Daddy calls his bad times his 'idiot spells.' He has them right regular."

"He's right about this being the last hanging," the Russell boy said.

"My daddy knowed the man they're hanging," another boy said. "He said that they ought to not hang him on account of the Bible saying that a woman ought to obey her husband when he tells her to do something and if she don't, you can kill her."

"I ain't heard tell of that," a different boy said, "but there's a heap in the Bible."

"It was the devil," Little Carl said.

The Bible-talking boy twisted his head and nodded and said, "Might have been." A couple of the others agreed with him.

"Where did you say y'all live?" one said like he might be coming out to see us.

"Out on Mr. Caudell's place."

Another boy, one named Benjamin, said that he knowed where that was on account of his daddy delivering feed out there. He explained to the others how to get to our place and I was starting to think I might better tell Mama we could have company.

A tall boy walked up about that time. His clothes looked a heap better than ours and a good bit better than the rest of the boys' did. They all said "hey" to him, calling him Ernie and I went ahead and done the same thing.

"Who is this?" Ernie asked them, pointing at me and Little Carl.

"Boys from out at Caudell's place."

"Oh," this Ernie said like that told him all he needed to know.

A boy said to Ernie, "Your daddy is letting you see the hanging?"

"Might as well," the tall boy said. "He was going to be here anyhow. He figured it wouldn't hurt for me to come and see him work. Mama weren't too keen on it, but he didn't listen to her on the subject." It turned out later that Ernie was the son of the man that was the preacher for the county, the preacher that would handle the religious talk at the hanging.

About that time, Daddy walked up behind me only I didn't know it. I was asking Ernie if having a preacher for a daddy made it harder or easier for him. Daddy slapped the back of my head hard enough to knock me into one of them saw horses. I grabbed ahold of it to keep from falling. "You rather be the son of a preacher man than the son of a working man?"

"No, Daddy," I started to say. I was trying to steady myself. He hit me with his fist in the chest and my breath shot out of me and my belly come up into my mouth.

"You take the 'little moron' and go sit with your mama."

As soon as I could breathe, I took Little Carl by the hand and led him over to the quilt where Mama and Gladys was still sitting. Daddy was watching every step, looking like he would draw blood if we didn't do as he said.

Once we set down, I could see him talking to them boys and I wondered what he was saying, but I didn't want to know. In a minute, they was all walking away from him and he was left standing there by hisself, looking at us. I knowed he thought it was our fault that them boys didn't keep talking to him, but it was something we couldn't help and didn't have nothing to do with, really.

Me and Little Carl set as still as we could there with Mama, me hoping the time would pass before we got into more trouble. A man come by in a little bit selling printed papers that told about the hanging. He said they was "programs" and that they would be worth a lot of money one day on account of there not being no more hangings. Them programs was three cents apiece, but folks was buying them anyway. I didn't see how no piece of paper could be worth that.

A good many folks did see it though, and bought his programs. One fellow standing beside us bought one and read it out loud to his wife and younguns, so I felt like we had got our three-cents worth without spending a penny.

Most of it was legal talk and then a prayer it sounded like for the little girls and their mama. Finally it had what the judge had said, I reckon, about Paul Tidwell being hung by the neck until he was dead. I was glad we hadn't spent three pennies on it because it weren't much of a story. You had to wonder why they didn't get somebody like Gladys to write them things. She could have made it a heap more interesting.

When the first bong of the First Baptist Church bell rung, it about scared me to death and I wasn't the only one. I think everybody on that square stopped and shivered and then realized it wasn't the Lord thundering, but just a plain old bell that had got their attention.

The bell rung eleven more times and everybody out there was looking at the gallows. We expected, I reckon, that the sheriff was standing there behind the door, waiting for the twelfth bong before he walked out with Mr. Tidwell. Of course, he weren't. The twelfth bong bonged and we stood there, looking and waiting, and nothing happened.

I reckon a couple of minutes went by with nobody saying a single thing. Finally I looked over at Mama. She was looking at Gladys, who was feeding the baby. I turned to look at Daddy, but he was just standing there all still and quiet like everybody else, waiting for that door to open, for the hanging to start.

I finally looked over at Little Carl. He was the only one that was looking at something else. He was turned slap around, looking past the buildings across the street, watching a dog that was hobbling on three legs. I can't stand to see a dog hurting like that.

We had a dog at home name of Jip. Daddy had got him to make a hunting dog out of him but he never did. Jip got to know Daddy pretty quick, I reckon, and didn't get around him if he could help it. Before Jip, we had another dog that we just called "Dog." It had got bad sick. Daddy said it had worms and he took and drownded it.

That dog hobbling on three legs was hurt and ought to have been killed. You'll hear some folks say "put it out of its misery," but a dog don't know misery, he just hurts. It takes people to know misery, to know that they are hurting now and always will. A dog just has this minute and this hurt. I reckon that's something a dog's got on a person, not knowing that the hurt ain't going to stop.

About the time I seen that poor dog, that big old door banged and creaked and swung open. The door was metal and I don't reckon it got opened a lot being as the only place it led to was the gallows. When that iron door hit the brick wall behind it, it banged so loud my ears hurt. Everybody in the street was looking, waiting for the show to start.

Two men come out wearing gray uniforms. I reckoned they was the deputies. One of them was toting a rifle and they both had pistols on their hips. A bald-headed man in a black dress come out right behind them. He turned out to be a judge, but he weren't the judge that had told them to hang Mr. Tidwell. He was a county judge and he was up for re-election that year so I reckon he was there to show folks that he was working.

Finally out come Paul Tidwell. Sure enough, he was a little bitty fellow with thick glasses. I expected him to look scared to death. I know I would have. He didn't, though. I would have been thinking about that rope and about being dead in a few minutes. He didn't look like he was thinking about nothing. They had his hands tied behind his back so he couldn't put up a fight, I figured. His feet was loose, but as many folks as there was around, there weren't no chance of that little fellow running and getting away. Folks had come for a good time and they weren't about to miss it if they could help it.

The sheriff, a fellow named Dave Mason, come out of the jailhouse then, right behind Mr. Tidwell. If you didn't know Dave Mason was the sheriff, you never would have believed it. He looked like a big kid hisself. He was one of them shiny faced men that didn't look like he was shaving yet, though you knowed he was. And even though he weren't no big fellow, he looked like a giant next to Mr. Tidwell.

Dave Mason had been to our house twice. One time, he had come to see if daddy knowed anything about some chickens that had gone missing from a neighbor's house. I was pretty sure Daddy hadn't stole no chickens, but I weren't plumb sure. Daddy liked chicken. The only other time we had seen the sheriff at our place was when he come asking if daddy would vote for him in the White Democrat primary that summer. I reckon Daddy said he would because Mason had left looking tolerable happy.

The day of the hanging, Mason didn't look like he much liked what he was doing. He looked around the crowd, looking as surprised as we had been by how many folks come to see the hanging, I reckon. Mr. Tidwell stopped walking in front of the two men with guns. Mason nudged him along toward the rope that dangled from the beam above them. There was a big metal lever there next to it. Mr. Tidwell looked at the lever and then up at the rope and then out at the folks that had come to watch him die.

Out the door behind them come Peter Tate, wearing a black suit and toting a book. The sheriff called him "Reverend" and had him come up and speak. Of all the folks up there on that platform, I think he was the only one that looked proud. He opened up the book he had with him, it was a Bible, I reckon, and said, "He that kill any man surely will be put to death." Then he done a prayer, asking God to have mercy on this fellow that they weren't going to have none on. I reckon Preacher Tate was doing his part and that he was expecting God to do his afterwards. When he finished praying, Tate told everybody to be sure to come to his church on Sunday so they could pray for Mr. Tidwell's soul. The sheriff finally pulled on his arm to shut him up.

Through all of this, the folks was real quiet except for some of the babies that cried every now and then. I kept expecting Little Carl to say something, especially when Peter Tate talked so long. He didn't, though. He just sat quiet, looking up at Mr. Tidwell. When the praying got over with and I had opened my eyes and looked, I would have sure swore I believed Mr. Tidwell was looking right straight at Little Carl, though we was quite a ways away.

When the preaching finally stopped, the sheriff said the legal things that I reckon he had to say. I didn't follow it and I don't reckon most of the grown folks did, either. Folks set and listened, but they were starting to get a little tired of waiting around and was ready for things to get going. When the sheriff finished talking, he turned around to Mr. Tidwell and put the noose around his neck. The little man moved his head to make it easier for Mason. The sheriff pulled the rope tight around his

As the rope was tightened around his neck, Mr. Tidwell smiled, I swear he did. The sheriff whispered something to him and stepped over to where the big handle was. I didn't have to understand the whole thing to know what that handle was for. That was what would kill Mr. Tidwell.

The little man spoke and he was loud. I hadn't expected that. I figured we were going to see him praying quietly. I don't know where I got that idea from.

"I killed the devil and then the devil got in me."

Like I said, he was loud when he said it. Nobody could have missed it: "I killed the devil and then the devil got in me."

Somebody in the crowd hollered "Hang him!" I couldn't tell whether a man or a woman hollered it. The sheriff held up his hand for folks to be quiet. Mr. Tidwell was looking at him then. The sheriff raised his eyebrows, wanting to know whether Mr. Tidwell had any more to say. The little man shook his head.

The sheriff had been toting a sack, I thought, only it turned out to be a burlap and wicker thing that he slipped over Mr. Tidwell's head. We wouldn't be able to see his face now. I heard Daddy whisper "damn" and I bet a lot of other folks done the same thing. That just weren't right. We had come to see a hanging and now they was going to hide the man's face. They might as well have it behind closed doors for what fun it was going to be now, I thought to myself.

The sheriff stepped away from Mr. Tidwell. The little man looked down then and I seen he weren't wearing no shoes, just a pair of socks. I wondered if they had took his shoes to make it harder for him to run off if he was to try and do that. The sheriff checked the rope over again and said to that deputy holding the rifle, "Do it." The deputy pulled the big lever and the floor dropped out from under Mr. Tidwell and he fell down through the hole and swung there.

Only he didn't die. He swung there, struggling because the rope was choking him. The sheriff looked mad and for some reason, he looked at Peter Tate like it was his fault that the execution didn't work. The little man weren't heavy enough or the drop weren't far enough. Whatever it was, it didn't break his neck like it was supposed to. He was just swinging there, kicking and jerking.

The sheriff trotted back inside the jail and in a minute come out the door below the scaffold. He went over to where Mr. Tidwell was jumping around. He hopped up and grabbed Mr. Tidwell around his waist and pulled with all his weight. That worked. Mr. Tidwell quit moving. His neck was broke. We couldn't really see it, but we knowed that was probably what had happened.

We all just stood there, all of us, looking. We was waiting for something, I reckon, but I don't know what. He was dead. The body swung a little bit and the rope squeaked against that beam it was tied to. It was so quiet, we could hear that squeaking way back where we was. Seemed like a long time passed and then a fellow from the crowd, stepped up under the scaffold and took ahold of Mr. Tidwell's ankle and looked at his watch. It turned out that was the doctor. The sheriff had to have a doctor make sure they had killed Mr. Tidwell.

The sheriff was standing there, waiting. The doctor looked at him and nodded his head and walked off. The sheriff looked around at all the folks. I thought he might say something about what had been done, but he didn't. He just looked and looked like he didn't much care for the attention. Finally, he went back into the jail.

I don't know what folks were expecting. I hadn't knowed what to expect, but I had figured that it would take longer for him to die. It hadn't took no time at all. It would have took less if they had got the roping right to start with. The hanging was over now and now they was left standing there looking at the body of a little fellow that had been just another sharecropper until a few months ago.

It was a disappointment for sure. The sheriff come out that upstairs door again, strutting like a man that's madder than a nest of hornets. The hanging hadn't gone like it was supposed to. The sheriff had the deputies go down below and when they got there, he cut the rope. The little man's body fell on the ground and the deputies put him on a little cart and pulled him inside the jail, out of sight.

The whole thing hadn't took no time. I wondered how many other folks had took off work like Daddy had and now was left with a day wasted. I heard a whimper and looked and seen Little Carl was crying. I didn't want Daddy to see him doing that, scared that he would whip him right here in front of everybody.

Somebody in the crowd hollered, "What you looking at, nigger?" We all looked around and seen a colored fellow standing at the back of the crowd, his white eyes wide and his fat pink lips hanging open. He dropped his eyes and turned away and started walking slow away from the place. I wondered if there might be another hanging.

A couple of the younger white men took off toward him and he begun to trot. They broke into a run and he did, too, and the next thing you know, everybody in the crowd was laughing at the sight. It was right funny.

We loaded up the wagon without talking. Daddy was mad like I knowed he would be. I kind of wished that they had caught the colored man and hung him because that would have made Daddy feel better. As it was, I was pretty sure he was going to keep thinking about it all the way home, the thing with me and them other boys talking and then the hanging going bad. He wouldn't blame me for it, it would just be that I had picked a bad day to mess up.

Mama got the baby and the croaker sack while us younguns got on the wagon. She handed the sack to me and the baby to Gladys. Gladys took the baby and opened up her shirt. We edged toward the back as soon as Daddy had the wagon moving. Little Carl whispered, "Tell us the rest of the story, Gladys." I didn't think that she would. I expected her to set quiet and nurse the baby and tell us to hush.

The baby got its lips pumping good and Gladys looked up and said, "I didn't tell you about how Mr. Tidwell got to Macon. That's what you might call another story, but it's a part of that first one, too."

"Tell it."

Gladys shifted so that she could nurse the baby and talk without being loud enough to get Daddy's attention. "Mr. Tidwell made it to Macon. He had a sister lived down there. He thought his sister would be able to help him. She had always helped him when he was little, but he hadn't seen her since she run off and got married when she was sixteen. He knew where she lived because she had wrote him a letter every Christmas since she left. He walked to Macon and found her house.

"Folks thought he might have had some help getting there and he did, but there wasn't no person helping him. Mr. Tidwell had the devil helping him."

Little Carl whispered, "I thought he did."

"The devil made it to where nobody could see Mr. Tidwell walking on that road. He walked along and a couple of dozen folks passed him, but not a one saw him. His sister Maggie lives two doors down from the Carver and Sons Funeral Home in Macon. When he found her place, he didn't knock or nothing, he just went in.

"Maggie had stayed home from the mill that day on account of one of her younguns being sick. She looked up at her brother natural as could be when he come in. She hugged him but didn't say nothing because she knew he wouldn't be there unless there was some trouble going on. She fixed him some cornbread and buttermilk to eat and told him she didn't have any money to give him and that her husband Ray would be home later and that he would need to leave."

"Did the devil come in the house with him?" Little Carl asked, like the devil might be some long-legged fellow that borrows supper and says you can come eat at his house, though you know you won't never do that.

"The devil didn't come into the house with Mr. Tidwell, but he waited outside. When the little man come out a little while later, the devil took right up and took him to the funeral home. The man there had a telephone that they used for business. He called and had Mr. Tidwell picked up."

"Why?"

"It was time, the devil's time. Everything comes in the devil's time."

I didn't say anything, but I thought about Mr. Tidwell's hanging. If there was ever a devil's time, that was it, it seemed to me. Anything shy of that was something else.

Gladys pulled the baby away and pulled her shirt back. The little thing was so full it was ripe to bust. She put it over her shoulder and patted its back till it heaved a little and giggled. She took to rocking it then and we stayed quiet, not wanting it to cry. A dark spot showed up on Gladys's shirt where the baby had fed and spread out from there. She had spots on both her shirts from the baby now.

She rocked it and rocked it. Finally it was asleep and I sure was glad to see it. The last thing we needed was that baby to start crying while we was on the road like that.

Little Carl was having a idiot spell, his mouth hung open like he was trying to catch flies in it. I didn't want to do nothing that would make him holler, but I was hoping that he would come out of it to where Gladys would finish the story. A bad bump in the road liked to have throwed us off the back even though we weren't going fast at all. That shook Little Carl and he looked around and whispered, "The devil's time."

"Yeah," Gladys said, "it was the devil's time for Mr. Tidwell."

"'I killed the devil then the devil got in me,'" Little Carl said. It scared me to hear him say that. It was like hearing Mr. Tidwell say it. It scared me.

Mama looked around then. I know she heard him and I figured daddy did, too, but he acted like he didn't. She give us all a look, Mama did, like to say we needed to be quiet because we knew what we would get if we done anything to get on Daddy's nerves. "'I killed the devil then the devil got in me,'" Little Carl said again. Then he lit up like he only did when somebody give him a piece of store-bought candy. "You know where the devil is now?"

Mama made a face at us. We needed to keep Little Carl quiet was what she was letting us know. Gladys poked her bottom lip out and shook her head. Mama's eyes said that we were on our own if daddy stopped the wagon.

"Do you?"

I whispered, "No," and that reminded Little Carl to keep his voice down.

He went back to whispering low, "Do you know where the devil is now?"

I shook my head.

"Devil don't stay with the dead. He come out of Mr. Tidwell when the sheriff broke his neck."

I wondered how in the world that little fellow, retarded like he was, knowed that the sheriff had broke the man's neck. I reckon he had heard us talk or just said it on account of the way the body swung.

Little Carl kept going, though. "The devil come out of him and come to us."

"Who?"

"Us," said Little Carl. "The devil is with us now."

His voice had gotten louder and it scared me. I didn't think about Daddy getting mad and turning around then. To be honest with you, I think I wanted him to turn around, to tell Little Carl to shut his mouth. He didn't.

"Mr. Tidwell was sad about dying, but he was happy to be shed of the devil. He looked at me and I could hear him saying it."

Gladys laid the baby in her lap. It was dead to the world, sleeping with little snot bubbles blowing out the side of its mouth.

Little Carl said, "We need the devil. Sometimes the devil straightens things out when God can't do it. God made the devil just like He made us."

I wanted to say that it didn't make any sense, but it did make sense. It made as much sense as anything I had heard anybody else say about God or the devil. Like I said, we weren't much for going to church, but sometimes you get stuck in a place to where somebody wants to tell you the good things Jesus has done for them, though I ain't never seen none of them folks doing that good. And I ain't never heard no real well-off folks thanking Jesus. They usually take the credit theirselves.

"Just what is the devil going to straighten out?"

"Ain't no telling," Little Carl said. He shook his head when he said it, like he was thinking about it and really couldn't fathom an answer. "Ain't no telling what the devil is going to straighten out, but I reckon he's coming to do it."

Gladys looked at Little Carl for a good little while before she finally said, "I don't know but that you might not be right about that, Little Carl. You just might be right." Derned if that didn't trouble me.

Little Carl was talking crazy and there Gladys went, saying there was something to what he had said.

We went by a colored man walking then. He took his hat off, stepping into the ditch and bowed his head down as we went by. I remember looking back at him and seeing that he kept his eyes on the ground till long after we were on by him. He knew better than to make a white man mad, especially my daddy, who had been known to whip a colored man out of plain meanness.

It weren't unusual at all for colored folks to get whipped if they got to acting up. Daddy said it was like raising hogs. Hogs is smart, but they forget they're hogs sometimes and will go to bite you when you're taking care of them. You can't put up with that or else the next thing you know, that hog will be doing it all the time and you'll have to kill him. It's better to whip them when they need it than to have to kill them, I reckon.

Daddy wasn't paying that colored man no mind as we went by. He was looking ahead and keeping the mules moving us on towards home. We was near about out of sight when the colored man finally put his hat back on.

There weren't much daylight left by then. We had wasted a good work day or the better part of it. I wondered if Daddy might not try to get some work done when we got home, though there wouldn't be a lot of time to do it. Working wasn't usually what Daddy done when he was mad, though. The longer we went along, the more I was sure he was mad about how the hanging had gone and whatever else he might be able to come up with that he could be mad about.

Gladys was done telling her stories and Little Carl looked like he had finished his, too. I laid down on the back of the wagon and looked up at the clouds, figuring that was the best way to keep quiet for the rest of the way home. Little Carl done the same and I was glad for that. Gladys looked like she had the baby resting good, too. The next thing I knowed, I had done gone to sleep.

Riding that bumpy road on the back of that wagon give me the oddest dream I reckon I ever had. It was a dream where there was a thunder rumbling that wouldn't stop. The wind was blowing hard and this gal with gray hair was flying in the air and I was flying with her. She was holding my hand and I sure did want to reach over and get a hold of her because she was the prettiest thing I had ever seen.

We was flying and the thunder was rolling across the sky and it was like we was riding on top of thunder. I could look down and not see nothing but black and I could look up and not see nothing but blue sky. I asked that gal where we was going and when I did, she turned her head and looked at me.

"He's bringing you home," she told me.

"Who?"

"Your daddy."

"All right," I said to her. She smiled and I could see her red mouth like it was really there, like it wasn't a mouth at all, it was a gash in somebody or some thing. It didn't scare me, though. It opened up like it wanted to take me in... and in that dream, that seemed like something good.

Chapter II
DEVIL

‑‑⟨⟩‑‑

I woke up with that roar of thunder fading out of my ears. I sat up and didn't see Little Carl. I looked around for him, but he was gone. "Carl! Little Carl!" I hollered.

Without turning around, Daddy said, "Shut the hell up. He's gone in the house." I realized then that Mama, Gladys and the baby were gone, too. I had looked for Little Carl because it was *my* ass if anything happened to him.

"You want me to help you with the mules, Daddy?"

I figured he would tell me he didn't my god-damn help or he might say it and then slap me.

He didn't though. He said, "How 'bout you go open the barn doors for me? Save me getting down."

I hopped off the wagon and ran the few feet ahead and opened the big wooden door. Daddy would unhitch the mules and take them out to the field and the wagon would be left inside, out of the weather. When the wagon had cleared the opening, I ran around and opened the other door so daddy could get out.

He was fiddling with the collar on Jack when I came back through. "What was Gladys telling y'all?"

"What?"

"I asked you what Gladys was telling y'all. I could hear her talking, but I couldn't make out what she was saying."

"She was making stuff up about Mr. Tidwell," I admitted. "She was trying to keep Little Carl quiet."

"Uh-huh," he said as he began to lead Jack and Johnny out. "You're full of shit." I didn't know why he was thinking I was lying. I wasn't. I was in for a beating, though, just the same. When Daddy got something in his head, you weren't going to get it out. You couldn't prove him wrong and you sure couldn't talk him wrong. For me, it was a matter of stand here now for a beating or run for the house.

If I stood here now and took it, it would be just as bad, but maybe he would let it go before he went inside. Maybe he would let it go with me and not whip Gladys and Mama.

Still, it was mighty hard to stand there and wait. "I ain't lying, Daddy."

He was out the door with the mules when I said it.

I waited till he come back in to say it again. "I ain't lying, daddy."

"Your sister's got a mouth on her, just like your mama does. You think I'm going to stand around and act like some kind of idiot like your brother, well, that ain't going to happen."

I didn't say anything back. I had already put some fuel on the fire without meaning to. He was bound to beat me now, though he probably would have anyhow. The hanging hadn't been as much fun as he thought it was going to be so he was mad about that. Whatever he thought Gladys had said just added to it.

I stood there and waited, hoping we could get this over quick instead of having it drawed out. When he was done with the mules and wagon, he looked at me like I was the biggest hog turd in the county. "You tell me what she said about me."

"She didn't say nothing about you, Daddy. She was making up a story."

"Uh-huh. Like I reckon you weren't telling them boys in town how sorry your daddy is and how you wish you was them."

"No, sir," I tried.

He kicked me in the stomach from where he was standing and I went flying backwards against the wagon. Daddy was on top of me then, slapping me across the face with his right hand. I don't know how many times he slapped me, I just know he didn't let up till he was out of breath. He was sitting on top of me and I couldn't hardly breathe.

"What did she say?"

"She told us that Mr. Tidwell got the devil in him. That's all."

He was breathing through his nose, looking down at me. "If you're lying, I'm going to kill you."

"I ain't lying, Daddy." I was crying.

He stood up and looked down at me. "Your damn idiot brother ain't never going to be no help to me and it looks like your mouth is going to keep you from being much help neither." He shook his head and spit on me and walked away. I was afraid he was headed in the house to beat Gladys, but I didn't have it in me to try and stop him. I laid there for a while, getting my breath back and moving slow to be sure wasn't nothing broke.

My face was hurting pretty bad, but not near as bad as my belly. I set up, but it sure did hurt. I thought maybe something was broke inside the way I felt. I breathed and coughed and caught my breath after a while. I knowed that the longer it took me to come into the house, the madder Daddy would be, so I tried to get myself up as quick as I could. I was taking too long and I expected to hear Daddy hollering, cussing at Mama or Gladys from inside.

I felt something lick my arm and looked around at Jip. He had come into the barn after Daddy had went out.

Jip had walked over to where I was sitting. He always looked happy except when daddy was around. He might have been a dumb dog, but he knew it wasn't a good idea to smile — or look like you're smiling — around daddy. He licked my face and I pushed him away. "Go on, dog. Git." He sat down and looked at me. He weren't going nowhere. He was making sure that I was all right. I weren't.

When I finally pulled myself up, I wiped off as good as I could. It wouldn't do to go in the house with dirt all over me, spreading it on Mama's clean floor. When I took a step, my side hurt like I had been kicked all over again.

Jip made the whining noise that he sounded like he hurt, too. His ears was down and he was wagging his tail real slow and looking up at me like he wished he could help me. There weren't nothing a dog could do, but it was nice of Jip to come to me like he done.

As I walked, my back hurt bad and I knowed I'd pee red the next day. That would happen if you got kicked in the back sometimes. It would take a while for it to quit doing like that.

I slipped in the house, quiet. Everybody was in the kitchen so I went to the bedroom first to wipe myself off good before going in there. I made sure there weren't no blood on my face or clothes. Daddy didn't usually hit you to where you'd bleed, but sometimes he done it accidental. When I was pretty sure I looked alright, I slipped into the kitchen.

Mama had made biscuits and streak-o-lean. There was a pot of collards going, too. If you put some pepper sauce on collards and daubed your biscuit in the juice, it was real good. Mama kept a hambone in the cabinet for the collards and I seen she had put it in the pot. Her cooking the streak-o-lean to go with it was something odd. I thought Mama must have made a good supper because she knowed Daddy would be disappointed by the hanging.

Daddy had set down to the table. He was grinning, looking at Mama and then at Gladys and then at Little Carl and finally at me. It scared me.

Somebody had brought in part of a Sears and Roebuck catalog and give it to Little Carl to look at and keep him quiet. I often wonder now what he was thinking about when he would sit quiet, looking at pictures of folks who was smiling and happy and had things that we didn't have and never would see.

Gladys was holding the baby in her lap. It was blowing bubbles, looking up at her. It smelled like pee, but it usually smelled like pee. If the smell got worse, Gladys would take it to the back and put it on a clean diaper. Daddy couldn't stand the baby messing up its diaper. Most of the time, he wouldn't pay it no attention at all. If it got to crying, he would get mad so we kept it as quiet as we could. Still, it was a baby and there just weren't much you could do with it sometimes.

Daddy was staring at Gladys and that made me worry. I was afraid it was her he was going to go after. He hadn't messed with her much since the baby was born. I knowed that wouldn't last forever. It was just a matter of time before her smart mouth would push him into whipping her again, baby or not.

"Didn't turn out like we expected it to, did it?" Daddy asked us and he smiled real big. I knew better than to answer. I made like I was interested in what Mama was doing at the stove. Daddy jiggled in the chair, sticking his tongue out and wiggling his butt to move that chair on the rough wood floor. "I figured we'd see him do a dance and piss his pants."

We laughed. I say we laughed, but I don't remember laughing myself. I just remember hearing somebody laugh.

Daddy kept grinning, looking around the table at each one of us, waiting. "I would have thought the sheriff was too old to play on a swing."

We nodded again but didn't none of us laugh this time. Mama said, "Supper's ready."

"What you reckon got in that sheriff, make him act like that? You reckon the devil got in him, too?"

"Come, get you a plate," Mama said.

"What you reckon we ought to do to the devil?"

Nobody said a word. Mama had give up on trying to head off whatever was coming. She stood there at the stove, but she was turned around towards us.

Little Carl didn't know no better and he spoke. "Kill the devil."

"Kill the devil!" Daddy hollered and then looked back at Little Carl. "That's what you ought to do."

Little Carl looked, but didn't say nothing else. Daddy got up and got two plates, put biscuits, meat and greens on them and sat back down. He passed one plate over to Little Carl. This was right unusual. Me or Mama would usually get Little Carl's plate for him. I got me a plate and Mama handed one over to Gladys. I went to eating as fast as I could. Sometimes when he was mad, Daddy would wait till you got your plate and then he'd slap it off the table and you'd go to bed hungry.

He looked at me between bites of collards and said, "What you thinking, boy?"

I knowed I had to answer him or he would bust me right then. I weren't able to stop what was coming but I might be able to slow it down, I figured. I said, "You reckon they'll hang somebody else?"

Daddy put his fork down and acted like he was seriously thinking about what had been asked. "I reckon they might. They used to hang niggers a good bit, but you don't hear of that as much as you used to."

Little Carl said, "Could you do it?"

"What?"

"Hang somebody."

Daddy was chewing a piece of the streak-o-lean, gnawing on the gristle, thinking. "Reckon I could," he said. And then he looked at the rest of us.

"You ever done it before?" Little Carl asked him. "You ever hung somebody?"

Daddy pulled the knottiest piece of gristle out of his mouth. "I helped a few times."

I didn't much figure that was true. If Daddy had ever helped at a hanging, he would have told us about it before. He was just making things up now, playing along with Little Carl. I hoped maybe he would calm down if this talking went on. It weren't likely.

"If he was the devil, could you could kill him, Daddy?" Little Carl asked.

"Yeah, I could kill the devil," he said. Looking at him setting there, I tried to picture it, Daddy killing the devil. All I would see, though, was other folks doing the killing, running up with axes and knives and whopping the devil while Daddy stood in the back behind them, waiting for his chance to join in after the devil was already dead. "I would make the devil do a dance and piss his pants!"

Little Carl laughed. I probably did, too, because I usually laughed if Little Carl did. It was like I was trying to cover his laugh up with mine so Daddy wouldn't hear it and hit him.

Daddy was sucking the last of the meat off the rind since he'd finished everything else. Gladys was still poking at her plate. She hadn't had much of a appetite since the baby. She had dropped off a good bit and it made her look a lot older than how old she really was. Daddy looked at her for a second.

She looked at him and he looked back at his empty plate.

"That baby's going to want some solid food before long," Daddy said.

Gladys looked up and then back down. She put some collards in her mouth.

"I said the baby's going to want some solid food before long," he said again. "You going to give it some of yours?"

Little Carl said, "It can have some of mine."

"I reckon I'll feed it," Gladys said.

"You ain't got nothing to feed it," Daddy said. "What you got there on your plate is mine. It ain't none of yours."

Little Carl had took his sweet time with his food and was near about through with it finally. I wanted to take him out of there, but I couldn't till Gladys left the table. My belly hurt and I wondered whether it was from the beating or from eating in such a hurry. She looked like she was in one of her woman-moods, as Daddy called them, and I knowed if I left her setting there, there weren't no telling what would come of it.

Daddy asked her, "What did you think about the hanging, Gladys?"

She didn't say anything back to him and that scared me. The only thing worst than saying something smart was not saying nothing at all. You could kind of see on her face that she had heard him, that she was being a smart aleck not answering him.

"I asked you what you thought about the hanging," Daddy said to her. "Did you think the devil had got in Tidwell? Did that sheriff kill the devil?"

Little Carl looked like he was about to say something and I jerked him by the neck and got his attention and he looked at me funny, but at least he didn't say nothing. Sometimes I swear I think it would have been easier to bring Jip to the table than Little Carl. The boy could cause trouble without meaning to and didn't have the sense God give a billy goat when it come to dodging it.

Gladys chewed her food slow, swallowed it and finally said, "I thought the whole thing was right funny, didn't you?" And then she grinned at him.

Well, he was going to slap her now, I thought. She brought it on herself with her smartness. Gladys took a bite of biscuit. I wished I could slip Little Carl out now, but there weren't no way to move before things blowed up. If Gladys was trying to make Daddy mad, she was doing a good job of it. His mouth was twisted and he was blowing breath out his nose so hard there was a ball of snot on the whiskers on his lip.

Gladys grinned real big then. "I said that I thought it was funny. Didn't you?" She asked him. "The devil died and we didn't even get to see it. All that trouble for nothing."

I pictured him slapping her across the face hard enough to make her head pop off. It wouldn't be hard with her little neck. Whatever possessed her to talk to Daddy like that, to grin in his face and push him, I just didn't know. She had been on the receiving end of plenty of beatings before the baby. She ought to have remembered what they was like without a reminder dose.

Just then the baby started crying. I wondered if maybe Gladys had pinched it to give her a reason to leave the room. She got up holding the baby and walked off from the table, still chewing the biscuit. Mama followed her.

After they was out of the room, I whispered to Little Carl for us to go on to the bedroom and get ready to go to bed.

Daddy hit me in the back of the head with his fist. "What the hell did you say?"

I shook my head. It hurt so bad I was dizzy. "I told him let's go on to bed."

"Like hell you did. You got a smart mouth, too. You just don't learn, do you?" I knew he wanted to hit Gladys, not me, but I didn't say nothing back to him. I looked down, hoping he was done with me for the day. "What did he say to you, Little Carl?"

My brother was bad about having his idiot spells right when you needed him to do something. This was one of them times. He sat there with a dumb look, like he heard what was said but didn't know how to say anything back. I couldn't help but think about the look that Jip had on his face a little while earlier.

Daddy looked at Little Carl and then back at me. I spoke up and said, "I promise you, Daddy, all I said was for me and him to go on to bed."

He hit me and I fell off the chair and into the floor. There weren't no whole lot of room right there so I couldn't get up too easy. Little Carl wasn't even looking my way so I knowed he weren't going to be no help and all I could hope was that Daddy wouldn't go to kicking while I was down there like that. I figured that after what I had got out in the barn, this was when he would finally kill me.

Mama come busting into the room then. I don't know whether she had heard him hit me or just got done with the baby. "Let him alone," she said.

Daddy jumped up from the table and turned around toward Mama. I was struggling to get back on my feet. I reached and took Little Carl's hand, hoping I'd get the chance to lead him out of the room while Daddy wasn't looking. Mama took a step toward me and Daddy hit her with the broad side of his hand right across the jaw. She slid down next to the wood stove that she had been cooking on.

I thought about what Gladys had told about Mrs. Tidwell falling against the stove and busting her head open.

That old cast iron stove was still real hot. Younguns usually learned to stay away from a wood stove the hard way and would have marks on their hands to remind them. When Mama went down, I was afraid she might have scraped against the stove and burned herself, but she hadn't. She was slow getting up and it looked like she might be hurt. The last time Daddy really hurt her, she was in the bed near about

a week. That had been rough on the rest of us but I knowed Daddy
wouldn't much think about that right then.

She finally teetered up and Daddy drawed back. "You get your
ass back in yonder," he hollered. "I'm teaching this one not to lie to
me."

Mama straightened up and looked madder than I had ever seen
her. "Ain't nobody lying to you," she told him. "If you would quit
lying yourself, well." She didn't finish. She held back from saying the
whole thing that was on her mind and I was glad. There weren't no
point in making Daddy no madder than he already was.

"I said to get in yonder!" he hollered at her. Then he turned back
toward me and Little Carl. I let go of my brother's hand and pushed
him, hoping he would get out of there while he could. Daddy reached
and grabbed my shoulder and started pulling me up. I shut my eyes
because I was so scared of what was coming next. As mad as he was,
he might very well kill me. I knowed that.

What come next though wasn't what I expected. Mama took the
stewer off the stove that still had the hot juice from the collards in it
and slung it on Daddy's back. He hollered like a hound and jerked
around, trying to get that hot wet shirt loose from his back. There
was enough grease in it that it stuck and burned him pretty good even
though it wasn't as hot as it could have been. It got his attention.

"I'll kill you!" Daddy hollered.

Mama turned and run out the door. Daddy was still struggling
with that shirt, but he was staggering out the door right behind her. I
knowed it would be bad when he caught her and I knowed he would
catch her. It was like Mama was dead already, running and knowing
she was dead and that sooner or later it would catch up with her.

I grabbed Little Carl's arm and we took off for the bedroom.
When we got in there, Gladys was holding the baby and grinning, but
she didn't say nothing. I set Little Carl on the side of the bed and took
his boots off of him and put him under the covers. He was tired from
the busy day and I figured he would go to sleep pretty fast and sure

enough he did. I would hear the baby squeak and stutter every few minutes, but Gladys didn't never say nothing.

Gladys ought to have knowed what would happen if she talked to Daddy like she had done. She knowed how Daddy was but she had got him going anyhow. I wondered if she had told the story on the wagon to egg him on. She was a right smart girl when she wanted to be.

I kept my boots on, afraid for what was going on and what might happen next. I set on the side of the bed like that a good while, just waiting and listening. Gladys and the baby faded off to sleep, but you never knowed when that baby might up and go to squalling and that would wake us all up.

I laid there and listened a long time. I figured that Mama might circle back and come running in and lock that door. That would end bad, too, though. Sooner or later we would have to open the door and I pictured in my head the devil being out there, waiting to come in. None of that never happened. Mama didn't come running in.

I reckon I was more tired than I knowed because I went to sleep. I didn't dream nothing this time, I don't reckon. I was still asleep when the sun come up and Little Carl got to moving around and woke me up.

Gladys was up already and feeding the baby. I must have slept pretty hard because she didn't wake me up at all through the night.

I got Little Carl's boots on him, took him to the outhouse and then me and him went to the kitchen. Usually Mama would have already been in there making whatever she had for us to eat. Weren't nobody in there that morning. There had been times when Daddy would beat Mama so bad that she couldn't or wouldn't get up the next morning and he would have to make his own coffee.

I was figuring on finding him in there that morning, but he weren't there. I had figured he would be setting there, drinking coffee with his hands still bloody from beating Mama to death. But he weren't there.

Weren't Mama nor Daddy in there. Gladys got a fire going in the stove. I asked her, "Where's Mama?"

"Don't look like neither one of them come home last night," she said. She set the baby down and took to poking at the fire with both hands, trying to get it hot enough to make coffee.

"Can we eat?" Little Carl asked.

Gladys didn't answer right off. "There's some streak-o-lean left over from last night if you want it." She looked at the mess in the floor. "Mama emptied the collards, it looks like. There was a biscuit left, but I done eat it."

Little Carl ate the meat. Gladys wound up making coffee and we all had a little of it. It was pretty good. Mama watered it down a good bit to make it stretch, but Gladys made coffee that would wake you up and send you to the outhouse.

After the coffee, me and Little Carl went to the well and brought in water. We done as much picking up around the house as we could. I cleaned up as much as I could from the mess them collards had made. The grease had left a dark spot on the wooden floor, but it sure weren't the first one.

We did all we could to make it easier for Mama when she got home. I had already started thinking "if" she got home instead of "when." I wondered what we would do if neither one of them come home. I didn't much figure Gladys wanted to raise three younguns. She was a youngun her own self.

I heard Jip bark. I run out and seen Daddy staggering toward the house. His overalls was soaked with blood and I knowed the minute I seen him that he had killed Mama. I didn't say nothing to him. I just got out of his way.

Daddy had the look on his face like it was all over. I hadn't never seen him look like that before. Usually Daddy looked like things was just starting and he was the one starting them. That day, though, he was a whipped man. He went past me like he didn't see me, went back to their bed and fell face down on it, dead to the world. He had done that before when he had worked the field so long it whipped him. It looked like the only thing that would whip him worse than work was killing.

We went outside, me and Little Carl, and done what other chores we could do. We fed the animals and cleaned up where we could. Gladys was busy with the baby most of the time, but she got the clothes together and washed as best she could out in the back yard with the pot and the lye. We helped how we could, bringing her what she needed when she told us. It was a scary day and we stayed as quiet as we could so that we wouldn't wake Daddy up.

We was hungry, but there weren't nothing ready to eat. There was some crackers and a little hunk of cheese so we eat them. That was about all there was right then that didn't need fixing. I wondered what we would do when Daddy got up. He'd be hungry. Gladys could come up with something good if she was of a mind to do it. I didn't know that she would.

I peeped into the room where Daddy was still laying in the bed. His bloody overalls had done stained Mama's nice quilt something awful and I knowed wouldn't nothing get it out. There was a big old spot of it there next to him.

When I went back outside, Gladys was waiting on me. "Mama may be dead or dying. If we find her and she ain't dead, maybe we can keep her alive."

I knowed she was right. "You going?" I asked her. I was afraid of being home with Daddy when he woke up and we weren't all there. He was going to be mad as the devil and whoever was still there was going to catch it.

"I got to stay with the baby," she said. "You need to go."

"What about Little Carl?"

"Little Carl?" Gladys said, "Do you want to go with your brother or stay here with me?"

"Daddy might wake up or Mama might need to be drug back to the house. I'm going to set on the steps." He said it like he had thought it through already, but that didn't make no sense at all. The boy couldn't hardly get hisself dressed, let alone think ahead to anything. "If either of you needs me, you can holler and I'll come running."

I remember looking at Gladys and thinking how Little Carl had surprised her, too. She said, "That ought to work."

I went outside and seen a drop of blood on the ground. Jip was asleep under a tree and he come over to me. He smelled the dark spot on the ground and then started trotting off, stopping and sniffing every little way along. I followed him. I watched him smelling the blood and trotting ahead. He stopped at the edge of the woods and turned back to look at me. I followed him and we went into the woods off to the west side of the house. Jip was bad to chase squirrels and I was afraid we would wind up standing at the foot of some oak tree in the middle of the woods, looking at each other and wondered how to get back to the house.

That didn't happen, though. We walked a good ways, him sniffing and trotting and stopping for me to catch up. We was far enough from the house that I felt like Daddy wouldn't be able to hear me. I started calling, "Mama? Mama?" every little while.

Jip stopped and barked. He hadn't barked since we left the house. Daddy had pretty much beat the bark out of him. I caught up with him and saw Mama's bloody apron laying there. Her scissors were all bloody, too, laying next to the apron.

Daddy had killed Mama with her scissors. Them scissors had been about the only thing Mama had that didn't belong to Daddy. They was the scissors that she used when she done her sewing. Her mama had give them to her when she got married to Daddy. When I seen them scissors, I knowed she was dead because she wouldn't have left them laying. I picked them up and put them in my front overalls pocket. Jip was looking at me and then he turned around and trotted further on.

I didn't know that I wanted to find Mama if I was going to find her dead. It was enough to know that she was dead and them scissors proved that. I didn't need to see her all messed up and bloody. My mind was drifting to hearing Gladys talking about Mr. Tidwell killing his wife and his little girls. I wanted to just turn around then and there and go back to the house and say she's dead and figure out what to do when Daddy woke up if he hadn't already.

But Jip was still sniffing and trotting and looking back, waiting on me to come on. I knowed I had to do it.

A big stump was where Mr. Caudell's property stopped. We didn't go into the woods too far because it weren't our property. Daddy had set rabbit traps along the edge of it the year before, but he had told us to stay out of it. Jip was trotting back and forth, though, letting me know that I had further yet to go. They must have gone past the stump because it was so dark they couldn't see it. I was sure hoping it weren't much further. I was scared of what I was going to do when I seen her laying there.

Jip barked and I looked up and seen Mama in the distance. She was setting on a rock there, not dead at all, but just setting. I walked towards her, still a little scared of what I would see when I got up to her. When I come close enough, I said, "Mama?"

She didn't turn around, but her head did move so I knowed she had heard me. I come a little bit closer and spoke again. "Mama?"

"I killed the devil," she said. "I killed the devil."

I run to her then, scared she was going to say that next part, but it didn't come. I put my arms around her from behind. She reached up, hugged me and pulled me around to her. She had been crying. One of her eyes was swole near about shut from the beating she had took. Her mouth was bloody and there was blood all over the front of her dress.

I seen then that she weren't cut or stabbed. She was hurt bad, but them scissors had had Daddy's blood on them, not Mama's.

Jip barked and started back towards the house. We followed him. Mama could walk, but she held on to her side the whole way. It was near about dark when we got back to the yard. Little Carl was setting where I had left him. When he seen us, he hollered, "Gladys! Gladys, come out here!"

Him and Gladys both come and grabbed Mama and helped her into the house. "Did he come back here to die?" Mama whispered.

"Yes, ma'am," Little Carl said. "He's in the bed in yonder."

We went in there and found him dead. Here, I had been looking at a dead man and didn't even know it I was so scared of him. Blood had soaked the mattress and oozed around the edge of him. It weren't Mama's blood. It was his. I leaned over and looked at his face, his eyes open just a tiny little bit to where you could see the dull dead shine. He scared me in a different way now.

"What are we going to do now, Mama?"

She was having to hold the wall to keep on her feet. "I reckon we got to tell the sheriff about him," she said. "They going to want to know what happened, who stabbed him."

"Will they hang you, Mama?"

She stood there, looking at him and didn't say nothing. I knowed she was glad he was dead. Well. I knowed I was. I didn't know what was going to happen next but it had to be better than what had happened before.

"They don't hang women," Gladys said.

"I reckon they might," Mama said. "They drawed a big crowd for that little Tidwell man. Ain't no telling how many folks would come to see a woman hung."

"They ain't going to hang you, Mama," Little Carl said. "You killed the devil."

Gladys said, "He was the devil. If you tell them what he did, there won't be nobody saying to hang you."

Mama shook her head. "People like a hanging."

We didn't say nothing else to that because we knowed she was right. The hanging we had seen wound up all messed up, but folks still had a good time. They might hang her just to get to see it.

We helped her fix supper. We didn't talk while we ate there in the kitchen. I reckon by then everybody was thinking about dead Daddy. I know I was.

I tried to remember something good about him because I felt bad that I was glad he was dead. I remembered sometimes when he would be busy working and I would help him and he acted like he was glad that I did. Then I remembered the day he kicked Little Carl.

We had been pulling weeds in the garden at the place we had stayed on before. The fellow there — and I couldn't say his name if I had ever knowed it — let us have a good-sized spot for our own to grow things on. He had helped Daddy with seeds and we had planted squash and okra and some other things.

Me and Little Carl was supposed to be pulling weeds out from around the little plants that was coming up. I was having a hard time myself knowing what was weeds and what weren't. They was all green and coming up about the same. I had turned my back for a minute to look at how far we had yet to go before we was done. When I turned back around, I seen Little Carl had got mixed up and was pulling up the okra plants instead of the weeds.

"That's the goddamned okry!" Daddy hollered. Little Carl weren't but five years old. He didn't understand. I was the older one and I really should have took better care of him.

Then I seen the big work boot hit his chest. He went flying and when he hit the ground, Daddy trotted right over and kicked him again. That kick hit him in the side of the head and his little neck made a pop when it jerked. I thought he was dead.

Daddy drawed back to kick him again, but the bloody spot on the little fellow's head made him stop. He picked him up and toted him to the house and put him in the bed. Mama was in the back yard working. I run out there and told her to come inside. When she seen Little Carl, she screamed and cried and held him. Her and Daddy fought right regular before that, but it seemed like the fighting got a lot meaner after Little Carl got kicked in the head.

For a while there, Mama and Little Carl slept together on a pallet that she drug into the kitchen. He got better, I guess, but he never was right again. He was slow, as they say, and sometimes he would have what Daddy called one of his "idiot spells," when he would stare at nothing with his mouth hung open and not say nothing.

Daddy didn't have a word for the other times, the times when Little Carl would act like he had good sense. The first time he done that, Mama thought it was a miracle cure, but it didn't last long. He went right back to slow and before long he had another idiot spell.

When I got a few years on me, I started to wonder what was going to happen to Little Carl. Was he going to be mine to take care of? Would he stay with Gladys? Turns out that I didn't have to worry none about Little Carl. But I'm gettin ahead of myself.

The night Daddy laid dead in the bed, I thought more about Little Carl than I did about the man that had hurt him so bad. Yeah, I had to admit it, I was glad Daddy was dead.

Gladys fixed some tea for all of us, she said, to help us sleep. We didn't have tea too much because Daddy didn't like it and wouldn't spend money on it. Mama had got some from a peddler that come through but she didn't let Daddy know about it. Gladys put a good bit of sorghum into the tea to sweeten it for us younguns, but it wasn't sweet enough to keep the hot stuff from burning our throats on the way down. She even give a little of it to the baby.

Mama slept with me and Little Carl that night. Gladys laid the baby down on a blanket in the kitchen.

When I woke up the next morning, Mama and Little Carl were still asleep, holding each other in the bed beside me. I got up and put my boots on and slipped out to the kitchen. The baby was laying in the floor, asleep still.

I looked around for Gladys, but I didn't see her. I went to the outhouse to do my business, expecting that I would find her there. It was empty, though. When I got back to the house, I got the bucket and went and got water from the well. I started a little fire in the stove to warm the water up with. We still had a good bit of wood on account of Daddy cutting so much in the fall and us having a warm winter.

I heard the door creak open and looked up to see Gladys coming in. She was filthy dirty and looked like she hadn't been to sleep at all. "I'm going to need you to help me."

"What?"

"I ain't going to let them hang Mama," Gladys said to me. She got the coffee pot and started putting it on the stove.

"How are you going to stop them?"

She didn't answer me right off. She was still thinking about the whole thing. "Daddy deserved to die. He ought to have died a long time ago. He ought not never been born."

I didn't say nothing back to her. She was right, but it wasn't something you could say. If Daddy hadn't never been born, we would have had a different daddy and the things that had happened wouldn't have happened. But you never knowed.

"You got to help me."

"All right." There wasn't really nothing else I could say. Whatever it was she needed my help on, I knowed I would have to help her.

"I got him hid in the woods past the field. He ain't much hid, but ain't nobody looking for him."

"What if a dog gets a hold of him?"

She hadn't thought about dogs. The county did have strays that would run a calf to death if they got a chance. As soon as the coffee was done, Gladys poured us both cups. I blowed it till it was cool enough to drink. We set there drinking it without talking. My head hurt and I figured out that she had put some of Daddy's liquor in the tea the night before.

Daddy weren't a big drinker, which is good I reckon because it might have made him even meaner, but he did keep a jug hid for when he might need it. Gladys must have slipped some of it to the rest of us to make us sleep while she was doing her devilment the night before. That was why Mama and Little Carl were still sleeping when they both usually got up before I did. If I had pondered it a little further, I might have figured out why that baby could be a sound sleeper sometimes and ornery others.

In a little bit, me and Gladys were stumbling across the field. It had been plowed one time, broke up to make it ready for planting. We got to the woods that separated Mr. Caudell's property from a piece that a fellow named Jenks owned. I didn't really know nothing about Jenks except that he had plenty of money and mainly worked colored and not white folks.

We weren't supposed to go into the woods back of the field, that was something Mr. Caudell had made clear to Daddy when he took us on as sharecroppers. He told Daddy there was a old well back there and a shack that had caved in. Mr. Caudell didn't want nobody going back in there and falling in the well and him getting blamed for it.

I knowed what Gladys had in mind. Instead of dragging Daddy around in the woods, I told her we ought to find the well first and then get him to bring him to it. We looked for a good while before we finally found what was left of that shack.

The whole thing had fell in and wasn't really to where you could walk inside. Somebody had took most anything worth taking from it. The top of it had caved in and the back side was the only part really still standing. "We could put him in there," I told Gladys. "Ain't likely nobody would ever find him."

She looked at it a good while before she finally said, "No, you was right to worry about dogs. Them dogs might get a hold of him and drag him up into somebody's yard. We put him in the well, that ain't going to happen."

We went back to where she had left him. He was face down on the bloody blanket that Gladys had pulled off their bed. He was stiffening up and his arms was bent all funny. I drug the blanket most of the way, following Gladys. As we got further in, she had to help me.

A old well was something folks didn't like to fill in on account of you might need it again one day. They couldn't leave it open, though, because a youngun or a grown person either one might fall into it. When we got there, I seen there was a piece of tin over it and a pile of rocks on top of that. We took the rocks off and pulled the tin out of the way. Up under there was some wood planks we couldn't see with the tin on it. I was scared there might be a snake down there so I kicked at it first. Didn't nothing move so I started reaching down and pulling the boards out of the way.

I finally could see the hole. I pitched a little rock in and listed for it to hit water, but I didn't hear nothing. I figured it was so deep that the noise didn't make it back up. That ought to work for Daddy. Gladys helped me pull him over there and slide him legs first into the hole. His arms caught, though and he didn't go all the way in. I knelt down there next to him and fiddled with him till I got his arms folded straight up. His eyes was still open a little and when I glanced at them, it was like he was still alive, waiting for me to not be paying attention so he could knock me down, kick me and then go after Gladys.

I gave him a push. He slipped down and out of sight. I pulled the tin back and then remembered the boards. I started over, putting the boards down first and then the tin and finally the rocks. Gladys was just standing and watching most of this. I reckon she was so tired that she just couldn't do no more.

We walked slow back to the house. I wished that Little Carl had been with us so he could get Gladys to telling a story. That would have took my mind off of the thing we had done.

"You was right," I told her. "We had to do it."

She didn't say nothing back, just walked beside me.

"If they knowed Mama killed him, they would hang her."

Gladys stopped and looked at me. "He weren't much of a man and he sure weren't much of a daddy. The things he done to us, he should have been killed a long time ago." I thought then how much she looked like Mama, especially since the baby had been born. They could have been sisters, they looked so much alike.

"Yeah," I said and nodded my head.

"He should have been killed a long time ago, but he weren't and now you and me got to do whatever we got to do."

"We have." I thought she was talking about hiding Daddy in the well. I hadn't really thought about what we was going to do next. She had.

She shook her head, "No, we ain't done much yet. We done what we had to do just now, but more is coming. You done good taking care of Little Carl. You going to have to do more, all of it, I reckon. I got the baby to worry about."

"What about Mama?"

"We'll see what happens next," she said and started walking again. "We'll see if Mama can do anything or not. She weren't the kind of woman to have younguns and she found a man that was even worse." She looked over at me again. "We got put in a bad place with bad folks and now we got to see if we can get out of it. Just don't count on Mama being much help. If she was, we wouldn't have been where we was at as long as we was."

These days, folks who move from up north to down here joke that "he needed killing" is a legal defense down here. It's a joke, but for folks like Daddy, it's true. I have thought a thousand times over that if we had gone to the sheriff and told everything that happened, I don't think Mama would have been hung. I was a youngun at the time, though, and I didn't know no better.

Chapter III
BARNESVILLE

We got to the house and Mama was up, sitting at the table, feeding the baby. Little Carl was next to her, a cup of coffee in front of him and that idiot spell look on his face. Mama looked up and seen us and then looked back down at the baby.

"Ain't no need for you to go to town, Mama."

"I figured that. I seen he was gone."

"You want to know?"

She shook her head. The baby had all it could handle. Mama put it on her shoulder and patted its little back and it let out a nasty belch and then it laughed. I laughed, too. I thought then that the baby didn't have no name and that wasn't right. It was a girl, I knew, but nobody called it nothing but "baby." Its little eyes wandered around the room and lit on me and I grinned at it and its eyes wandered some more.

"He run off," Gladys said. "Anybody ever asks, we tell them he run off. Men run off all the time. I don't much figure anybody is going to doubt it nor go looking for him."

"I don't reckon we can stay here," Mama said, looking me and Little Carl up and down. "It would be rough trying to make a go of this place with just two boys and two women trying to do it all."

"You got kin," Gladys said. "You got folks that would take you in if they had to." I hadn't never thought about that. I hadn't never had cause to. It was one of them things that if I had of thought about it, I might have thought about it a little too much. I might have thought that we could have done something different long before we done it.

If we tried to stay on Mr. Caudell's place, it wouldn't last long. When he seen that Daddy was gone, he'd likely cut us off at the store. Daddy probably owed Mr. Caudell money on top of all that. Being a sharecropper meant you borrowed all the time just to get by and then worked and worked trying to pay it back. I knowed that when a month or two went by and he seen that Daddy weren't coming back, he would probably be on us to move so he could get a new sharecropper on the place and ready for planting season.

"You ought to drag that mattress to the trash pile and burn it," Mama said, all the time looking at the baby and not at us. "It won't burn easy nor quick. You need to soak it good with kerosene before you light it. It needs to be burned good before anybody sees it or knows your daddy is gone."

We drug the mattress out back to the place where Daddy had burned our trash. It was a stinking pile of ash and broke bottles and cans. We flipped the mattress on top of the pile with the bloody side up. I done like Mama said and took a bottle of kerosene and let it soak in real good. Gladys put the trash from the house around the mattress, poking it under where she could so it would all burn and be mixed up.

It went up with a "Whoomf!" when Gladys lit it. I stepped back and watched it burn. With the kerosene and that cotton ticking, the fire burned like it was alive, like it was mad and crazy and trying to get aloose from the mattress so it could go and get ahold of somebody. Fire can make you watch it, I swear it can. It can make you forget you're just watching.

I stood there a good while. Little Carl was standing next to me and I didn't know how long he had been standing there. The mattress was burning, but it had slowed to mainly smoke and stink. The cloth had burned off a lot of the cotton pad, but the blood had soaked into the cotton pretty good. I wondered if there was any way it would ever burn.

That mattress smoldered a long time. I finally got a stick and poked it and spread the cotton to where it would burn, but even then it was slow going. Little Carl didn't say nothing the whole time, just stood and watched.

When Gladys come out, she brought me some water and a biscuit. Little Carl followed her when she went back inside. I just kept standing there, making sure that mattress burned.

About half of the mattress was gone when I finally set down on the ground to watch it. I wound up going to sleep, holding my head in my arms on my knees. The fire went out after a while, but the smoke still come up from it. I reckon one of us ought to have thought about the smoke that thing was going to give off, but we didn't.

Little Carl woke me up, telling me to come to supper. I didn't think it could be that late, but it was. The stink of that burning, bloody cotton was so strong on me that I went and washed off by the well before I went in to eat. It didn't work and I knowed I must smell awful to everybody else because I smelled awful to me.

I reckon Mama had cooked near about everything we had. There was canned beans and tomatoes and hoe cakes and some ham. We hadn't eat this much since Christmas, but I figured I knowed why we was doing it. We couldn't stay there forever. We couldn't stay there for long at all. We would need to go somewhere else. We wouldn't be able to tote much with us and it would be foolish to walk off from all that food.

Or maybe she had fixed it to be a reward for us, a special prize for me and for Gladys for cleaning up the mess she was in.

We set down and got to eating. Gladys was feeding the baby some mashed up beans mixed with a little tomato. The baby seemed to like it pretty good. Little Carl was eating hoe cakes with ham and not paying the beans no attention. I wasn't having no trouble cleaning my plate neither. It was good. Mama could flat cook when she set her mind to it and had something to cook.

We was near done before she told us, "I got a sister in Barnesville name of Clara. I don't know if y'all remember her. She ain't been to see us in a good while but her and her husband Henry are good folks. Clara will help us out if she can."

I sure didn't like that part about "if she can." It made me think we might get there and find out that they couldn't help us, they *wouldn't* help us, and that they would wind up calling the law on Mama.

"We get up early and get going, we can get there before dark," Mama said.

"We going to walk all the way to Barnesville?" I didn't really know how far that was, but I worried about the trip for the four of us and hauling our things with us, though there weren't no whole lot of things to take.

"We might get a ride with somebody," Mama said. "Folks will feel sorry for a woman and younguns walking. We might get a ride take us part of the way."

The "mights" was thick in what Mama said and that worried me. Even with that, I knowed we was better off than we had been with Daddy. Most anything would have been better than that when I thought about it.

"I ain't going," Gladys said then.

We all looked at her.

"You can't stay here," I told her like I had anything to say to anybody about what they could do or what they couldn't do.

"I ain't going," Gladys said to us again.

"Caudell ain't going to let you stay here," I said. "You can't work this place. Even if you could, you got the baby to take care of. There ain't no way Mr. Caudell is going to let you stay on."

"I ain't going."

I started to say something else, but there weren't nothing else to say. I wondered if she was saying that she weren't going to try and keep Mama from leaving, but that weren't the way she was acting.

Mama folded her arms like I had seen her do when her and Daddy would fuss. I half expected her to draw back and slap Gladys, but she didn't. She set there looking at her like you would look at hogs when it was getting cold weather.

The chair Daddy would set in was empty. If I had thought about it at all, I would have moved it before supper. Now it was setting there making me think about him all over again. Mama and Gladys didn't say another word.

Mama got up and took Little Carl's plate back to the stove and refilled it. "You want anything else?" she asked me.

My stomach had gone from empty to full of knots in just a little while. I knowed the smell from that fire was still mighty heavy on me, but I didn't think that was what was messing up my appetite. It was thinking about leaving and not having Gladys going with us. She was a youngun herself. She couldn't stay by herself.

We finished eating. It took me a while to finish, but I finally did. Little Carl had finished two full plates and was eating one more hoe cake. I don't think we had ever set down and eat that much at one time.

"You think you can stay here?" Mama said.

Gladys said, "Uh-huh. I think so."

They looked hard at each other and I did not have no idea in the world what they was thinking. Gladys couldn't stay by herself. Mama couldn't leave without her. But here they was. Mama got up and left the table and put things away and started packing up what we would take with us the next day.

"Maybe we could ride instead of walk. We could take Jack and the double-tongue wagon," Mama said. "We could send him back when we get settled in in Barnesville."

Gladys shook her head. "Johnny ain't no good without Jack and Mr. Caudell wouldn't like it a bit if anything happened to either one of his mules."

Mama twisted her mouth around. I couldn't believe she was letting Gladys tell her what to do. I figured it was on account of Daddy being in the well that Mama didn't think she could make Gladys behave no more.

"You could load up that wheelbarrow Daddy used to use for seed and take it."

I thought Mama was going to swallow her lips. Finally she said, "I reckon we could do that."

Little Carl got up and headed to the outhouse. I got up and went on to bed and he come in there when he come back inside. We took off our boots and overalls and laid down. It was hard to think of how things was going to be without Daddy. I was used to being afraid of getting whipped if I done the least little thing wrong. I was used to getting whipped if I was just in the wrong place when he was in a bad mood. It don't make sense how you would get used to something bad like that, but you do.

I was thinking about that when Little Carl asked me, "What did y'all do with Daddy?"

I started to tell him, that's how dumb I was about things right then. I stopped myself, though, and I said, "We buried him."

I expected him to ask me where or something, but he didn't. He turned over and went to sleep. I laid there for a while, thinking about all of it, wondering what would happen if this happened or if that happened. I thought about going to jail and wondered what that would be like. I had heard about folks going to prison, but I didn't know nobody who had been and who had got out.

When we got up the next morning, Mama already had loaded the clothes we had into a croaker sack and put that into the wheelbarrow. She had throwed other things on top of that and had put some food on there for us, too, and a jug of water.

Little Carl had got up and got ready on his own. We had coffee and biscuits and cheese. We went by the outhouse and then met up with Mama in front of the house next to the wheelbarrow. Mama was wearing the only dress she had besides the one that had blood all over it. She was wearing a broad hat pulled to where the bruising on her face weren't too easy to see. She took the handles of the wheelbarrow and started down the road, me and Little Carl following.

I remember Gladys standing there, holding the baby and not saying bye or nothing else when we went walking out of sight down that dirt road. Little Carl turned around and waved at her and she waved back, but we kept going. The wheelbarrow looked like it might tip over at first, but it settled as we went and by the time we got down the road good, it rolled fine.

It had started off a pretty morning, but it started clouding up when we left the house. There weren't another house between us and Mr. Caudell on the corner of the dirt road and the state road. It started sprinkling rain and I thought for sure Mama would have us turn around and high tail it back for the house, but she didn't. We just kept walking on and in a minute it quit. I reckon it was good that the clouds and little bit of rain did come because it kept us from being so hot.

Walking past Mr. Caudell's house was risky on account of us having his wheelbarrow. He might see us, come out and holler at us and make us give it back. He would probably ask about Daddy, too, and I reckon that was the biggest thing we had to worry about. I kept thinking how he didn't like to talk to women and would probably talk to me and I wouldn't know what to say. I hoped that maybe he wouldn't be like that and would talk to Mama.

We walked by his place and I couldn't take my eyes off of it for fear that he would come out and I wouldn't see him coming. The place was a farm house, bigger and nicer than ours, but still just a farm house. You could see the wood where the paint had come off on a good bit of it and I remember thinking that if I got to be big enough and old enough and was still around here, I might offer to paint it for him for enough money to get Mama something nice for her birthday. That was a right crazy thing for me to be thinking right then. I reckon I was thinking that maybe some good things could happen just like some bad things happened.

Mr. Caudell didn't show up, though. I walked along there, expecting that he was in the house, looking out the window. That was dumb of me. Mr. Caudell weren't no rich fellow letting other folks work while he set back and made the money. He worked, too. He was out plowing a field hisself that day, working a pair of mules just like Daddy would have done. I didn't think that through. I thought the man was setting up there in his house.

About the time we had walked out of sight of his place on the state road, Little Carl come to life and started talking, asking Mama questions. It was one of them times when he would act like there weren't a thing in the world wrong with him. I remember Mama would cry sometimes when he done that because she knowed that as pretty as you please he could slip back into a idiot spell the next minute.

"Is Aunt Clara going to be glad to see us, Mama?"

"I reckon," Mama told him. "But I ain't seen her since" She had to think about it. "I ain't seen her in a long time."

"What does she look like?"

"Well, she used to look a lot like me, but I reckon she looks a heap better than I do now. She lives in town and has it pretty good. Her and her husband Henry used to come see us when we lived on the McElhaney Place, but your Daddy run them off on account of something Henry said."

Now I was kind of thinking about the whole thing and asked her, "You ain't seen her in so long, how do you know where she lives?"

"Well, I'm hoping she ain't moved since Christmas. You remember she sent me that letter at Christmas."

I remembered Mama getting a letter. It was the only time I could remember her getting mail. She had read that letter two or three times real slow. I knowed she didn't read too good, but she made like it was Aunt Clara's writing that she was having trouble with. Daddy got mad at her for reading it over and over and snatched the letter out of her hands and put it in the stove and burned it up.

Then Mama looked down at Little Carl and said, "I don't reckon you remember, but she did, she wrote me a letter, telling me that they live in the mill village up the road from the buggy factory."

"Buggy factory?"

"Yeah, her husband Henry works there and sounds like he makes good money. That's why I'm hoping that she can let us stay there with them for a while."

Little Carl asked her, "They make bugs?"

Mama grinned and I think it was the first time I had ever seen her do that without catching a fist for it. "No, honey, buggies. You know, like horses pulls for fancy folks. It's a wagon folks ride in."

Little Carl still didn't understand, but he quit asking about it. He went on to the next one. "Why didn't Gladys come with us?" I was glad he asked that because I was wondering it myself.

"Gladys is a woman now, with a baby she has to take care of," Mama said. "She's doing what she thinks she needs to do to take care of her youngun."

That didn't make no sense. Gladys had a baby, but she weren't no whole lot older than I was, I didn't think. I didn't know how she was going to make it without Mama nor Daddy there.

I even thought maybe I ought to have stayed there to help out, but I knowed Mama needed me. There weren't no way I could do both. If Gladys needed help, she ought to have come with us. Mama had let her have her own way, though, which would have been crazy if it had been me or Little Carl wanting to do it.

He asked her, "Are you going to get a job making buggies?"

"I don't think they hire women at the buggy place, but I figure I might get on at the cotton mill. I've heard tell they pay pretty good."

"Does Aunt Clara work there?"

Mama shook her head. "Aunt Clara don't work."

"She ain't got no younguns?"

"No, her and Henry ain't never been blessed with none."

Little Carl was having a good day right then because he didn't say anything back about that. We all just kept walking. I wondered about Mama saying "blessed" about having younguns. She sure didn't act like Gladys was blessed when she had her baby. The whole time before that baby was born, Mama acted like it was the worst thing in the world.

We walked by a field where there was some colored folks working. They looked around at us, but they didn't say nothing. I looked to see if there might be a white fellow running things — there usually was — but I didn't see none. I wondered what Daddy would have said about them being left on their own like that. We walked on a good ways.

I asked her, "Can I push the wheelbarrow for a while, Mama?"

"If you want to, sweetheart, but you let me know when you get tired and I'll go back to pushing it."

So I pushed it the next while, listening to Mama answer a bunch more questions that Little Carl had about Aunt Clara and Barnesville.

Was she older than Mama? Yeah, but not by much.

What did Uncle Henry look like? He was just a regular looking fellow, but he had been in the Navy and had a tattoo on his arm of a anchor.

They went on and on and I quit listening. I was looking ahead at the road because it didn't look like it had no end and we seemed to be walking slower than we was when we started.

"Y'all move over to the side," Mama said to us. "Yonder comes a wagon."

Sure enough, a wagon pulled by two mules was coming up from behind us. Seemed like it took a while to catch up, but when it did, we seen that it was two men and a woman riding. The woman was setting between the two men. The man driving pulled up next to us.

They stopped along side us and the woman hollered, "Y'all need a ride?"

"We ain't got nothing to pay with," Mama said.

"That's all right," the woman hollered back. "I'd appreciate the company. These two ain't said a word since we left the house." She cackled laughing like she had cracked the best joke you had ever heard.

"We're going to Barnesville," Mama told the woman as we hoisted the things out of the wheelbarrow and then flipped it wheel-side-up onto the back of the wagon.

"Well, that ain't far. We got to go all the way to Macon."

"You got people in Macon?"

"A sister," the woman told us as we climbed up onto the back of the wagon. She looked at me and said, "Why don't you sit up here with the men-folks. I'll ride back here with your mama for a while."

I looked at Mama and hoped she would say for me not to. She said, "Go ahead, son, it's all right." So I climbed up there between these two men that I had never seen before in my life and away we went. The one wasn't no whole lot older than me and he was driving. The other one smelled like sweet tobacco and I wondered if he had a pipe in his pocket or if the smell had just stuck itself to him whether he was smoking or not.

I couldn't hear what was being said in the back, but I tried. I knowed the woman had to be asking Mama about who done that to her face, but since I wasn't able to hear it, I didn't know what was being said exactly. I figured Mama wouldn't let on about Daddy, but it worried me a sight that Little Carl was setting back there with them. Weren't no telling what he might say.

The two fellows sitting with me didn't say a word the whole time and I didn't say nothing either. Neither one of the smoked or dipped while we rode. We rode a good ways. It was still cloudy, but it seemed like it weren't going to rain any more. About the time we went by a crossroads, though, there was a rumble of thunder behind us.

"Sounds like trouble," the older man said. "You ain't got trouble following you, do you, boy?"

"No, sir," I said to him. I knowed he was just making a joke about the thunder, but I didn't like what he said. Thunder and lightning scared me back then and sometimes it still raises my hackles.

There was another rumble then and it was closer. The man driving jiggled the mules on. It didn't matter. It thundered again and the rain started beating down on us, right into our face like it was trying to get us to stop. The man driving took the mules off the road and under a tree close by and that took most of the rain off of us. We set there for a while, waiting it out. I got onto the back with Mama and Little Carl and the woman got up on the seat with her folks. When it finally did quit raining, the woman moved back with us, but she didn't say nothing to me about moving to the buckboard. I was glad to get to set back there with Mama and Little Carl.

"Won't be long before we're in Barnesville," the woman said. "I wish I had brought some cards and we could play cards while we ride."

"I ain't played cards since I was a youngun," Mama said and smiled. I knowed what cards was, I had heard tell of people using them to play games, but I didn't know nothing else about them. Daddy had talked about playing cards before he met Mama. He told it like playing cards was something that was bad on account of him losing a lot of money when he done it.

"Well, if I had some, we would play!" the woman said again like she was real happy about something that wasn't going to happen no how.

Mama shook her head. "They is a whole lot of things I ain't done since I was a youngun."

Till she said that, I don't reckon I had ever thought of Mama ever being a little girl. I didn't really know nothing about her besides her being my mama. But she had been a little girl and then a woman that got married to a man that wound up beating her. I didn't understand how she wound up like she had, but I couldn't.

"My grandma on Mama's side was a full-blooded Cherokee," the woman said. "She said how grown folks had to keep some of the childishness in their hearts."

I thought that was a right dumb thing for somebody to say, even a Indian. I thought about Little Carl. There was a fellow who was going to be childish for the rest of his life. That weren't no way to be.

Little Carl was listening to the women talk, but he wasn't saying nothing. I was glad for that. The woman was telling Mama about a man she knew in Barnesville that had a hardware store. The man's wife had died and he was lonesome, the woman told Mama. I wondered how the woman knowed so much since she didn't live in Barnesville, but I kept my mouth shut.

Mama said she didn't know nobody in Barnesville except for her sister and Henry. "I hope I can get me a job in Barnesville," she told the woman. "I'm hoping somebody will give me a chance to work for them and show what I can do."

"Well, you need to meet Mr. Hearn. He's a fine Christian man and he would be happy to meet somebody that would appreciate him."

Mama said, "I'll talk to Clara about him and see if she knows him."

"Well," said the woman, "he's a good Christian man."

I didn't know what she was trying to say, calling the man a good Christian. The woman agreed with Mama that that her way might be the best way of handling it.

The woman started talking then about her son, the man who was driving the buggy. She was right proud of him for working at a feed store in Zebulon for near on three years and saving enough money to buy his own wagon to deliver goods on for folks. This trip to Macon was a chance for her to see a cousin that she hadn't seen in ten years and a chance for Tom, her son, to see if there might be more money to be made there than in Zebulon.

The woman kept talking a good while and I started hoping it would come up another cloud to shut her up. I was so scared that Mama was going to say something or that Little Carl was going to say something and all of us would wind up in the hot water.

We started seeing houses here and there and I knowed then that we was getting close to town. I didn't know how long we had been on that wagon, but I knowed we would still be hoofing it way back up the road if them folks had not come along. We went by a little store that looked like a house somebody had took the notion to nail a bunch of signs onto.

The man driving the wagon stopped and handed the reins over to his daddy. He went inside the store and was gone for a good while. We just set there quiet, waiting on him to come back. There was a rumble of thunder off in the distance. In a minute, the driver come out and we took off again.

"I'm going to take y'all on to the buggy factory. You won't be too far from where your folks live. We'll be turning off toward Macon right past there."

"Much obliged," Mama said. "Y'all have been real kind."

"Weren't no trouble for us," the woman said. "I was happy to have a woman to talk to. Them two don't talk enough to keep a body company." She laughed a little bit and Mama smiled again.

When we got to the turnoff a few minutes later, Tom stopped the wagon and we got down. The woman's husband helped put our things down and load the wheelbarrow back up. The woman and Mama hollered bye to each other till the wagon was out of sight.

We were left standing there on the street heading into Barnesville. There was a sign in front of the building that made buggies. We stood there for a while, Mama trying to figure out what to do.

The buggy factory helped us out then. There was a whistle that blowed and the fellows come out of the place a minute or two after that. Mama stood there, looking at each one of them that come by us. Finally a fellow come out and looked at her and she looked at him and she said, "Henry?"

He grinned back, shook his head and said, "Clara's been talking about you, wondering how you was doing. I thought I was going to have to ride over there and whip your husband just to satisfy her wondering."

Mama said, "We need a place to stay, me and the boys. I hate to ask you, Henry, but you're all we got."

That stopped him. I reckoned he was going to tell us to start back for home, that he didn't have room for us at his place, but he didn't. "We ought to be able to figure something out," he told Mama. "Come on."

Mama walked ahead of us with Uncle Henry and we followed, me pushing that wheelbarrow. They didn't talk on the way, just walked and looked. I kept looking at him, wondering about that tattoo he had, but I couldn't see it because his shirt covered it up.

Barnesville had some nice houses and I got to admit, it didn't look real to me. It was like looking at pictures out of the Sears and Roebuck catalog except these houses was bigger and old. We was walking along with the other folks from the buggy factory that lived in our direction. I said, "Do you live in one of these houses?"

Uncle Henry laughed and made me feel foolish for asking, but I still weren't sure of the answer. I thought at first he had laughed because I ought to have knowed it was his house, but later on I figured out it was because I ought to have knowed it weren't.

We walked past them big houses and walked by stores and such until we come to some more houses, only these was smaller and newer than them others had been. Folks started dropping off then, hollering, "See you tomorrow" or "Bye for now" or such as they went off toward the house they lived in.

We turned and walked down another street a ways down. All the houses were alike, but the folks had different things out in the yard. Some of them had little gardens. Some had chickens. One of them even had a car. We stopped there and Henry told us that the man who lived there had bought the car second hand from a fellow in Atlanta, but that he wasn't able to drive it and had parked it there in the yard for the past few months.

"This is it," Henry told us when we got to their house. It was a plain little place, but it was a good bit bigger than the one we had lived in at the Caudell place. Henry hollered, "Clara! Clara! You got company!" when we got to their yard.

In a minute, a woman that looked like Mama except younger come out and run to Mama. They hugged and went in the house. I pushed the wheelbarrow on and Uncle Henry walked us to their house.

Mama and Aunt Clara stood there, hugging and crying. "Did you leave him?"

Mama didn't say nothing back to that. "He's gone," she finally said. We all went inside then, but I left that wheelbarrow on the porch.

Their house was nice. The inside was all painted and there was a couch and a chair in the front room. It was a pretty good sized room and I wondered if one of them slept in there. Uncle Henry told me and Little Carl to follow him and we did. There was two doors at the back of the room. He pointed with his thumb and said, "That's our bedroom."

He opened the other door and said, "Y'all can sleep in here." We went in and seen a mattress laying on the floor in one corner and a cot in another. "My mama and brother slept in here when they come back at Christmas. That cot ain't big enough for but one. I got it from the

Sears catalog. That mattress there was here when we moved in. We turned it over and it sleeps pretty good, from what my brother said."

I didn't know what to say. I knowed I didn't need to say nothing. Henry was being mighty nice to us, considering he didn't hardly know Mama and sure didn't know me nor Little Carl. Uncle Henry had a hard-looking face but his eyes give him away. He weren't hard. I seen right off that him and Daddy wouldn't have got along.

I heard Mama then. "Y'all bring our things in from the wheelbarrow."

Henry toted most everything in. There weren't no whole lot as I looked at it. We had a spare pair of clothes for me and Little Carl. Mama had her night gown and some women's stuff and that was about it. It put me to mind of just how much of nothing we did have. Here Mama was coming to stay with her sister and didn't have much of nothing to her name.

Our room was painted and fixed as nice as the front room was. Besides the cot and mattress, there was a little chest of drawers in there that Henry said had belonged to his granny. We put everything in it and still had a drawer left over. They had a picture of a little boy and a sheep on the wall and Mama said that was a picture of Jesus. I didn't figure it was, though. It didn't make no sense for him to be squatted down next to a sheep.

Aunt Clara fixed supper for us. She made hash and put onions in it, which I didn't think I would care for, but it turned out good. We had great big biscuits and pinto beans to go with that. There was mashed potatoes, but Aunt Clara called them "creamed" on account of putting milk in them, I reckon.

We ate our fill, but there was more left when we was done. "It'll be in the icebox if y'all want some more later on," she told us. There weren't no way I would have gone back and eat more. I knowed they was being extra nice to us right then, but if we didn't act right, they would put us out. That's how folks do. Even knowing that, it was hard for me not to slip back out there and have me a hash biscuit because they sure was good.

After we finished eating, Mama and Aunt Clara set at the table, talking. Uncle Henry showed us the outhouse, which was a lot nicer than the one we had had. They had a bucket of stuff that they put down in it regular, he said, and that kept it from stinking so bad in hot weather.

We got back inside and Uncle Henry said, "You boys are going to have to work around the house to pay your way. You understand?"

I didn't say nothing and I'm glad I didn't. When he said that about work, I thought about Daddy and the work that he done and the work he had Mama do and had us do.

Uncle Henry made a face at us, looking at us like he wanted us to know he meant business.

He said, "First thing every morning, I want y'all to take the slop jars out of both bedrooms and go empty them in the outhouse. After you do that, wash up real good and bring in some water from the well for your Aunt Clara."

Well that weren't much. That weren't much at all. "Yes, sir," I said to him. I wondered if there was something else he would expect us to do later on or if he thought I weren't right neither.

He grinned and went on, "And after we eat supper in the evenings, I want y'all to clear off the table. You ain't got to wash dishes, but you clean up and put the dirty dishes in the sink for your Aunt Clara. You reckon you can do that?"

We said we thought we could. He grinned again. He knowed what he was giving us to do weren't no whole lot, weren't really worth doing as jobs went, but it was something. I think he come up with them things just to make us feel like we was earning our keep, though I knowed we weren't.

When he got done talking to us about chores, we went back to the porch, the three of us, and set down on the steps. It sure was a nice place. I wondered if Uncle Henry could get me on at that buggy place. I would have done whatever they told me to do. I figured I would need to show Uncle Henry that I could work first and ask him to get me hired on after while.

Little Carl hadn't said nothing in a good while and I wondered when he would come back to life and hoped he didn't show out since Henry was being so good to us.

"Little Carl, you don't say much, do you?"

"He got kicked in the head," I said.

"Yeah. I heard tell about that," Uncle Henry said and give Little Carl a long, hard look. "Did they ever get a doctor to look at him?"

"No, he didn't bleed no whole lot," I said. "Mama kept a poultice on it for a while till it quit running off. It healed up pretty good, I reckon, but he started having his spells after it."

Uncle Henry rubbed his hand through Little Carl's hair and I knowed he could feel that knot the little fellow had had since he got kicked. You couldn't see it on account of his hair, but you could sure feel it if you run your hand across it. It was like how folks will try to fix a dish or a jug that's got broke, but it don't never fit back together just right. There's always a little bump. That was how Little Carl's head was.

I said, "Sometimes he talks like there ain't nothing wrong with him, but then he has his idiot spells and gets like this."

Henry leaned over and hugged Little Carl and I thought that sure was nice of him. I couldn't remember nobody but Mama ever hugging him before. I swear I believe Little Carl grinned, but that sure ain't likely. Uncle Henry said, "You boys ever been to school?"

"No, sir," I told him. "Daddy said it was a waste of time for a man to set and not do nothing when there was work that needed doing. He said men that goes to school gets uppity and ain't worth a flip when it comes to working."

"Uh-huh, that sounds about like him."

I said, "You going to make us go to school?"

"Well, it's about over for this year," he said. "They don't run it during the summer, but you might ought to go come fall."

"Uh-huh," I said. I wondered if he thought we was going to be there that long. I reckoned he did. I hadn't thought about it. I hadn't figured they was going to let us stay at all. The idea of staying there in that nice house was mighty appealing except for the talk about going to school.

He grinned at us and it made me feel like he liked us. I don't really know why he would, but I reckon he didn't have no younguns so he didn't know how troublesome we could be. He said, "You want me to read to y'all?"

A couple of times I had had folks read to me from the Bible and I didn't much care for it. If they told you a story, that was fine, but most of the thing didn't make no sense. The fellow reading it would read it and then tell you what it meant but didn't none of what he said match up with what he had read. It just made you wonder if he knowed what he was reading or whether he was just making it up to fit a idea he had.

"I ain't much on the Bible," I told Uncle Henry and then regretted it. I was letting my mouth run when I knowed I ought to keep it shut. I didn't need to be telling the man that was letting us stay in his house that I didn't want to hear him read the Bible if that was what he wanted to do. I could have a idiot spell my own self if I didn't want to listen while he read it. "If you want to read it out loud, we'll listen to it."

"It ain't the Bible I was planning on reading," Uncle Henry said. "I got some books with stories in them and I thought I would read y'all a story if you wanted to hear one."

"I like stories," Little Carl said out of the blue. "I like to hear stories."

Henry went into the house, back to their bedroom and come back out with a book that had pictures of rabbits in it and he read it to us. I didn't much like it because I didn't like how the rabbits acted and how the pictures showed them wearing clothes and all. It didn't make no sense to me, but Little Carl liked it so much I thought we was going to have a hard time when it was over.

"That was good," Little Carl told him. "That was real good. I bet them little rabbits acts better now!"

Uncle Henry laughed at what Little Carl said, but he didn't draw back to hit him or nothing and I was glad for that. "You want to look at it some more?"

"I guess so," I told him and me and Little Carl set on the steps till dark looking at the pictures in that book. I reckoned if somebody could think up rabbits wearing clothes and talking, they could think up most anything and maybe there would be a place in the world for Little Carl even if he did have his idiot spells. Little Carl just set and looked at them pictures over and over again. He would grin and turn back and turn ahead. I just set and looked at him, thinking how glad I was that this made him happy.

Mama called us in and we went to the room they had for us. Mama and Little Carl took the mattress and I laid down on the cot. I was more tired than I knowed I was and I went right to sleep. I woke up early the next morning, wanting to take out the slop jars as soon as I could to show them that I was going to do my share of work.

The slop jar in Uncle Henry and Aunt Clara's room was empty and there weren't nothing but a little pee in the one in our room. I remember feeling bad about that, like I had got cheated out of a chance to do more. I emptied that one and washed it out and took it back inside.

Aunt Clara was setting at the table talking to Mama when I come back inside. They was having coffee and grits with cheese in it. It was pretty good. Mama's eye looked a whole lot better. Mama looked a whole lot better. She was wearing a dress that I reckoned Aunt Clara had got for her. Uncle Henry had done gone to work at the buggy factory. He left about daylight, they said.

"I'm going to walk with your mama up to town and see if we can get her on at one of the mills," Aunt Clara said. "I know some of the women that works at them. It ain't the best jobs in the world, but it pays and it's regular."

Mama was fixing her hair then, combing it to where her bruised eye wasn't as noticeable. It was more like a mix of shadows now than a black eye. It turned out they had put some powder and some paint on her face to cover up that bruise. It was hid real good.

"You look pretty, Mama."

She grinned, but she was scared. I reckon she was scared about trying to get a job. She went to comb her hair again, but Aunt Clara said, "It looks fine. You keep combing it, you may mess it up. Leave it."

Mama done like she said and sucked in her breath and her eyes blinked. "I ain't never done nothing like this before. I never had a job except farming and raising younguns."

"They show you what to do and you do it. You think Henry was born knowing how to make buggies? He weren't. He got that job there and they done moved him up to doing a different one. He's doing fine at it and you'll do fine at the mill, too."

It sure was good to hear somebody talking so nice to Mama. I started to say something, too, but I couldn't think of nothing that would make any sense. I didn't know nothing about working at the mill.

"If you get that job, we going to get Gladys, ain't we?" asked Little Carl.

"Gladys don't want to come with us, son," Mama said. "She's making a life for herself like grown folks have to do."

"She ain't grown."

"I know she don't seem like it to you. Sometimes she don't seem grown to me neither, but she is. And your brother'll be grown before you know it and then it will just be me and you."

"And the devil," Little Carl said and it about scared me to death when he did.

Aunt Clara said, "The devil?"

Mama was shaking her head and saying, "No, no, no, Clara. He's touched. He's not right. He says things that don't make no sense."

Little Carl started to say something else, but Mama raised her hand toward him and he stopped.

She said, "We done left the devil behind. You ain't got to talk about the devil no more."

Little Carl said, "It don't matter whether we talk about him or not."

"Then we won't," Mama said. She tried to act like nothing was wrong then and said, "Clara, I'm sorry, but the boy ain't right and he says things that don't make no sense."

"Yeah," Aunt Clara said and then looked down at Little Carl. "Well. We need to get going." I think she was happy to step away from him right then.

"We'll be back as quick as we can," Mama said to us. "Y'all don't get in no trouble while we're gone."

"What you want us to do?"

Aunt Clara smiled at us. "You don't have to do nothing but play. You can play out in the back yard or sit out front and watch folks walk by. I like to do that myself. Just don't leave the yard. We don't need y'all getting lost."

"We ain't going nowhere," I told her.

They started off, walking toward where we had come from the day before. Aunt Clara turned back and said, "If y'all see a snake, get away from it. Don't try to kill it, just get away from it."

I hadn't even thought about seeing no snake. We would see them sometimes at Mr. Caudell's place, but I never thought about snakes coming through town, coming down busy roads, coming to houses like these was. Made me wonder.

Little Carl went over to the tree and looked at it like he wanted to try to climb it. There weren't no limbs low enough for him to reach so I knowed that wasn't going to happen. He set down in the dirt and started picked up the acorns and sticks and little rocks and the next thing you knowed he was all busy trying to build something.

I was thinking we needed to be doing something useful to where Uncle Henry wouldn't be in no hurry to put us off the place. Since Little Carl was playing good by hisself, I went walking around the house, looking for something to do.

Their house faced the little road that run through the mill village. We'd see folks walk by here and there. Most of them would wave and holler "Hey" at us if they seen us. A few would scoot by like they was in a big hurry. When we had lived at Mr. Caudell's place, we didn't hardly never see nobody. Being in Barnesville showed me what it was like to be around so many people.

I liked it for the most part, but I kept wondering what Gladys was doing. I hoped she had changed her mind about staying there and was on her way to catch up with us, but I didn't reckon she would know where we was. There weren't no whole lot left at the house for her and the baby to eat. I had to just wonder why Mama would let her stay there by herself. It didn't seem right to me.

My mind was back there with Gladys but my feet was in Barnesville. I looked down and seen where somebody had started building a little rock edge at the front of their yard, something to separate it from the road. I got to studying on that.

I went back to where Little Carl was and he was still stacking sticks and things, building little houses in the dirt and having a good time.

The roots of that oak tree were all over the back yard and in spots, they had pushed rocks up out of the ground. I started going around to the rocks that were sticking up and prying them up where I could. When I got two or three good-sized ones, I toted them around front and put them in line with the other ones along that line.

Little Carl got interested in what I was doing, but without saying nothing, he just started doing it, too, only he was using a stick to pry at the rocks and before you knowed it, he had popped up some pretty big ones. We toted and pried for a good while and finished the whole line of rocks on the front edge of the yard close to the road.

It weren't much, I knowed, but we had done a little something. I was especially proud of Little Carl for working and doing like he had. Soon as we was finished with it, I seen Mama and Aunt Clara walking towards us. They was talking and as they got closer, I could hear Aunt Clara saying that it wasn't her that had got the job for Mama, it was Mama herself. When they walked up, I think Mama was about as happy as I had ever seen her.

"What happened, Mama?"

"I'm going to be working at the bleachery."

I didn't know what that was, but I was glad it made her happy. I was hoping she would see the rocks me and Little Carl had put out, but she wasn't paying no attention to us. Aunt Clara saw it, though, and said, "Look at what these little fellows have done! They finished that rock outline I started back last fall!"

Mama weren't paying no attention, but Aunt Clara went on and on about how good we had done.

"What is the bleachery?" Little Carl asked her like he had good sense.

"It's part of the mill where they bleach the cloth," Aunt Clara said. "They make it pretty and white before they send it off to be made into clothes."

"You know how to do that, Mama?"

"They going to teach me how to do it, the man said. He said he could use somebody that wasn't scared to work hard and I told him I wasn't. He hired me on the spot."

"Your mama starts tomorrow. She'll be able to go in with Henry and come home with him while y'all stay here at the house with me."

"What are we going to do?" Little Carl asked her. "Will you read stories to us?"

Aunt Clara kind of grinned at him, but it was a real sweet grin, not like how Daddy would grin before he slapped somebody. She said, "I don't read as good as your Uncle Henry does, but I can try."

"You think you can find some more books about them rabbits that talk and wear clothes?"

"I think I can. We thought we was going to need them a few years back and your Uncle Henry bought some books for younguns, but it turned out we didn't need them," Aunt Clara said. I didn't know then what she meant and wondered why you would think you need books and then not need them.

I didn't much like the idea of setting around all day long and having her read to us. I reckoned if I could show them how good a worker I was, they would help me get on at the mill or at the buggy place. If Aunt Clara could take care of Little Carl, I could go get me a job and make some money for us.

When Uncle Henry got home, he sent me and Little Carl to the back yard and then he set down with Mama and Aunt Clara and talked with them a good while. Me and Little Carl set under the oak tree back there, building little houses with the sticks and acorns he had piled up before. Little Carl started telling a story to go along with our playing, telling about them talking rabbits and adding some more little animals that talked and wore clothes.

We didn't really pay no attention to the grown folks. Used to have been that if we got sent outside, we'd set and look at the house for when Daddy come out in case he was mad and looking for us. Now, here we was, setting there, playing. It was right odd not having to worry about getting whipped all the time.

I looked at Little Carl and thought he was a whole lot sharper than I had ever figured him to be, coming up with that story about them rabbits and all. His story kind of wandered around a little and never did have no ending, but it was good enough that I remembered it and thought about it that night when I was going to sleep.

Mama stuck her head out the back door and hollered for us and we come in. Aunt Clara had made a pot of pinto beans and a pan of cornbread and that was what we had for supper. Uncle Henry cracked some jokes about tooting and Little Carl laughed.

When we went to bed that night, Mama stayed up later. She said she was too scared to sleep and wanted to talk to Aunt Clara and Uncle Henry some more. Me and Little Carl laid in the bed and talked a long time. I asked him where he got them stories he had told and he said they was just something in his head that come out when he got to playing.

I told him that I wished I could make up stories like that, but he said I couldn't do it on account of the things I had to do that he couldn't do. I laid there and thought about that a good while. Then I didn't want to think about it.

"You miss Gladys?"

"Uh-huh," Little Carl said.

"I do, too," I told him. "I wish she would come here, come and live with Aunt Clara and Uncle Henry."

"She can't," Little Carl said. "The devil is busy with her."

I didn't say nothing back to that. I just looked hard at him, wishing he wouldn't talk like that.

"Mama left her there to slow the devil down."

"Gladys ain't got nothing to do with the devil."

"All of us got a little something to do with him," Little Carl said. "You can kill the devil, but the devil gets in you. He got in Gladys and he got in Mama and —" But Little Carl didn't finish and I didn't want him to. I figured I knowed where he was headed.

In a minute or two, I heard him snoring. He had done gone to sleep. I didn't go to sleep that night for a good while.

That cot was sure nice and I reckon when I did finally go to sleep, I slept good. When I woke up the next morning, I was in there by myself. Mama had done to work and Little Carl weren't nowhere to be seen. I put my clothes on and trotted to the kitchen and there he was setting at the table with Aunt Clara. They was eating and she pushed a chair out for me to take and I did.

It was good, but I don't believe we ever had a bad meal with Aunt Clara. There was always plenty and it was always good. I was setting there that morning, eating my breakfast when it hit me that I had forgot about them slop jars. I jumped up to go empty them, but Aunt Clara told me to eat first, that chores could wait.

I eat and then I went and emptied them, but I sure felt bad about it. One little thing they had give me to do and I slipped up and didn't do it. Aunt Clara didn't let on that she was mad, but she must have been.

She wouldn't let me help her a little while later when she went to wash clothes out in the back yard. She said for me and Little Carl to go play. I told her we would be glad to do some work for her but she said that we needed to play. That was on account of her being mad at me for forgetting the slop jars, I'm pretty sure.

I took Little Carl and we went and set on the front steps of the house. We got to looking up and down the street, sizing up the folks that we seen here and there. There weren't many men walking the street because they was at work. It was mostly women and a few old men. I kept hoping that we might run up on some boys our age, but we didn't see none. Two or three times, girls come by, but we didn't holler to them like we would have if they had been boys. We just watched them and they didn't pay us no attention.

We'd been setting there a good while when this fellow with a nice suit of clothes and a hat and big mustache come by us. He looked hard at us, like he was fixing to say something about how we didn't have no business being there, but he kept walking and went to the house next door to Uncle Henry's. He didn't knock or nothing, he just opened the door and went in.

He come back out a little while later and walked like he was in a mighty big hurry back towards where he had come from before. He didn't look at us at all that time. I didn't really think nothing about it, but Little Carl said how it was funny that the fellow didn't stay long after coming on such a long walk to get here. I don't know how he knowed the fellow had walked a long way, but I thought the same thing after Little Carl said it.

The next day it rained. It didn't rain much. It weren't no gully-washer, but just a little dripping rain. Aunt Clara got out some books and read them to us and then told us to set in our room for a while and look at them. I had of rather been doing some work, earning my keep, as they would say, but there weren't much to be done on a rainy day.

I was thumbing through one of them books, looking for pictures, when Little Carl called me over to the window. Our room was right across from the bedroom window of the folks that lived in the next house, the house that the fellow with the mustache had been to.

Little Carl said, "Look a yonder." He pointed toward the house next door. That house was so close that you could see right into the window during the daytime. They had curtains but they had forgot to pull them shut and from where we was, you could see right through the gap in them and into the bedroom there. There was a man and woman on the bed naked, going at it. The man still had his socks on and Little Carl thought that was the funniest thing in the world.

Where we lived before had been a little place and we had seen Mama and Daddy going at it a couple of times, but it wasn't like this. Mama and Daddy stayed under the covers.

These folks weren't staying under the covers. They was all over the bed and onto the floor and up against the wall. They was having a good time, too, squealing and laughing and tumbling.

I don't know how long we watched them, but it must have been a while. When they finally finished, the man hurried and put his clothes back on and left. We seen him come out and go trotting down the street toward the mill. "Old Socks sure is in a hurry," Little Carl said and that made me laugh harder than I think I ever had or ever will.

After a while, that woman got up and put her clothes on and went out of the room and we couldn't see her no more. Me and Little Carl got the same show near about every day about that same time if we remembered it. The man would go in over there and the next thing, they would be going at it. Old Socks was a right regular fellow when it come to that.

When Sunday rolled around, we slept a little bit later. There was still chores to do, but breakfast was bigger and we ate supper earlier since wasn't nobody at work. Mama and Uncle Henry had the day off from work, so they set around, resting and talking. I was scared they was going to want to take us to church, but didn't nobody say nothing about it. I asked Uncle Henry if he was a church man.

"I used to go right regular," he said, "but since we moved here, we haven't found no church that we like."

I said, "Uh-huh," but what I thought was "You got to like it?" I thought that would be a hard thing to find unless there was one that had service later in the day and fed you on top of that.

Late in the day, Mama asked them if they had any cards. Uncle Henry grinned and said that he reckoned they might. He went looking and come up with a deck that was tied together with twine. Him and Mama and Aunt Clara got around the table and he snipped the twine with his pocket knife.

"I ain't played cards since I was a little girl," Mama told them.

"That's all right," Uncle Henry told her. "I ain't played since before me and Clara got married."

Aunt Clara admitted that she might have played cards with Mama when they was little but she didn't even remember it.

The three of them set there, fiddling with the cards until Uncle Henry come up with what he could remember about playing poker. He dealt the cards out, but he had to keep on reminding them of what to do. "Might be better with four playing." He looked at me and Little Carl. "Y'all want to play?"

Being asked to play cards puffed up my chest something big but Little Carl jumped in the chair before I could and I wound up being his helper instead of him being mine. I have to admit that I didn't follow poker too good. You got cards and then you swapped some of them and then you would show which ones you wound up with.

Little Carl got pretty good at it and was playing better than Aunt Clara by the time they quit. Uncle Henry said they could play with matchsticks and pretend it was money and they done that a good while. Mama told Little Carl that he couldn't keep his matchsticks when it was over and he would have to give them back, but that didn't bother him none. He grinned and said, "You ain't going to have none to give back!" and they all laughed.

I remembered what Daddy had said about losing at cards. I reckoned he had played for money and not for matchsticks. I seen where that would make the game a heap more ornery than playing for matchsticks did. Knowing how Daddy got about other things, I figured he probably would have fought over cards a good bit.

When it started getting late in the day, they quit playing and started getting ready for nighttime. Me and Little Carl went to the back yard to use the outhouse, but we stopped and looked through that window to see if Old Socks was there. Old Socks weren't there, but there was another fellow, a skinny man with a nose that made him look like he had a bird's head.

"If that other one is 'Old Socks,' this one here is 'Pecker,'" Little Carl said and we both snickered. We must have been a little too loud because Pecker looked in our direction and come over and closed the curtains and that ended our show with Old Sock. We would still see him come and go at the house, but we didn't get to watch the going at it that went on in between.

Pecker would be there on Sundays and Old Socks through the week. One time Pecker come over to talk to Uncle Henry. We was scared he might be telling on us, but it turned out that he was asking him about Old Socks, but Uncle Henry didn't tell him nothing.

I can't tell you how good that was, us living there with Aunt Clara and Uncle Henry. Mama was working and as hard as it was, it weren't nothing compared with how she had been on the farm. Didn't nobody beat her in Barnesville. Didn't nobody cuss her or whip her children bloody or nothing like that. Her face healed up pretty good from the last beating Daddy had give her. She had a scar above her left eye and a big bump up under it. Aunt Clara said that bump was where the bone broke and healed crooked. Mama said it didn't hurt much except when it rained.

Barnesville had a parade on the Fourth of July and we went to see it. They closed the mill and the factory for the day so everybody could go. Folks used to seeing a big parade might not have thought much of that one in Barnesville, but me and Little Carl thought it was the grandest thing we had ever seen.

We watched the fellows in their old army uniforms come by and we waved at them. Next come probably a dozen different fancy buggies that the factory put in the parade. Each one of them had somebody setting up top and waving and a sign on the side that said who they was. We couldn't read it, but Uncle Henry would tell us what they said.

We waved at all of them, but it was always right funny when some fancy looking person would be waving and all the while one of them horses was dropping turds right in front of us while they walked.

We waved at all of them. Everybody did. Even the horses pulling the buggies acted like they was having a good time, stepping high and turning sometimes to look at the crowd of folks that was waving and hollering.

One of the last buggies that come by was carrying the Parade Queen, according to Uncle Henry's reading of the sign on it. We looked and riding up on top of that thing was this woman wearing a fancy dress and a crown and waving to beat the band. I don't know what a real queen acts like, but that woman sure acted like she thought she was the real thing. Setting right there next to her was Old Socks, grinning and waving like he was the Queen instead of the woman setting next to him. It didn't hit me then that it was his wife setting next to him. I'm glad it didn't or I might have busted out laughing.

The Klan come by, all serious and scary, wearing their sheets and hoods and holding up signs telling folks who they ought to vote for in the Democratic primary later that summer. Some of them had pulled their hoods up on account of it being hard to walk and see out of them two little holes, I reckon. We waved at them and even though they was supposed to be serious and scary, a good many of them waved back.

Then come some more, the Masons and Oddfellows and the Sons of the Confederate Veterans. All of them marched along waving and smiling. Some whistled and a few hollered and all in all every one of them seemed to be having a real good time.

Aunt Clara had got up early that morning and fried a chicken and made a bunch of biscuits. After the parade, we went to the field where folks was gathering, spread out a blanket and set down and eat. It was mighty good and after it was done, a fellow wearing a right ugly red-white-and-blue suit come by with peppermint candy for all the younguns and told the grown folks to be sure and vote for Bacon in the election. We laughed at that, thinking the man meant the kind of bacon that you eat, but Uncle Henry said it was a fellow by the name of Gus Bacon that was running.

After the food was all gone, I thought we would be going back home, but there was one more thing yet to see. There was a big music show on the square with folks singing and playing guitars and banjoes and fiddles. I had not heard no whole lot of music at that time, but I liked it. We wound up listening to a bunch of them sing and play. Most of them played music like they play at church, but some played music that I liked.

Toward the end, a band that had a young fellow from Philadelphia, Pennsylvania — I remember on account of him saying it two or three times and laughing every time that he did — played a song called "All She Gets from the Iceman is Ice." It made the grown folks, most of them anyway, howl laughing. I don't think I ever seen Mama laugh so hard. When it was about over, the sheriff come up and made them stop playing it, but he was grinning, too, so I figured he was just making them stop as part of the show.

The last bunch that sung didn't have no music to go with it. It was just these four fellows that would raise and lower their voices and make goo-goo eyes as they went. Some of their songs were right funny the way they did them. Near the end, they done what they called a sacred song about a baby sheep's blood. The last thing they sung was "Dixie." Now, near about every group that had got up there that day had sung it, but these fellows done it with just their voices and it was so pretty you would have thought angels was singing. When they got done, everybody clapped and clapped.

It took us a good while to walk home on account of all the people that was on the street. I was put in a mind of that hanging. It was a right interesting the way folks had acted at that show, but this one was better to my thinking. Nobody got hung, but everybody looked like they had a good time. Little Carl had learned some of the words to "Dixie" and sung it over and over on the way home, trying to do his voice like them fellows in that last bunch had done.

When I think back to it, that Fourth of July may have been the best day of mine and of Little Carl's life. We laid in the bed that night and talked about it. Uncle Henry come in there to tell us we needed to go on to sleep, but he wound up setting and talking to us hisself for a good while.

"You ever join the Klan, Uncle Henry?" I don't know why I asked him about that instead of the Masons or the Oddfellows, but I did.

"I thought about it," he said, "but I don't reckon I'd be too good at the kind of thing they do." I remembered Daddy talking about wanting to join the Klan except he didn't have enough money to pay for the sheet and hood. To hear Daddy tell it, the fellows that run the Klan was using it to make money, not to do what it was supposed to do.

Little Carl asked him, "Did you see the Queen?" Of course, he had seen her. He was the one that had told us who she was from that sign on her buggy.

"Yeah, that's the mayor's wife," Uncle Henry said. "They make her the queen of the parade every year. I don't know whether the mayor got her made queen or whether she got him made mayor."

Little Carl tried to sing "Dixie," but by then he had done forgot how it went. Uncle Henry sung it through for him, trying to help him latch on to it. Little Carl sung it through twice and Uncle Henry finally said he was going to "give up the ghost" and he went to bed.

I went to sleep that night hearing Little Carl singing that song over and over and over. He would make his voice shake when he sung "away" and I thought he was about to cry, but he weren't. It sure did sound good, even though he was just a little boy singing it and not one of them grown men that done it in the parade. Like I said, I believe that Fourth of July may have been the best day we ever had.

The fire at the mill, and I reckon you've read about that before, happened later in the week and for the folks that was used to seeing parades and hearing music, they probably didn't remember the Fourth of July after the fire.

There had been a spell of dry weather and then a storm come in. It rained about all day on Friday and was still raining Saturday morning when Mama left for work. The bleachery didn't have but two working doors and both of them was on the west side of the building.

Mama went to work like any other day, back to her place pulling wet cloth through the big wringer. She was always careful about that machine on account of it hurting so many folks who had worked that job before her. She said it was right easy for it to twist the cloth and pull a arm into it if you didn't pay attention to what was going on. If you was to get your arm caught in that thing, it would mess you up and you wouldn't be able to work no more.

She was back there pulling the cloth through, which she had decided was a lot safer than trying to untangle it as it went in. When she heard the floor boss holler, she thought it was on account of somebody else getting hurt or falling behind in what they was doing.

He wasn't hollering at anybody, though. He was hollering at the sky and when Mama looked around, she seen lightning shooting everywhere out the big windows. A bolt hit the tin-roofed shed that was on top of the building. That set the little wood shed on fire and that fire caught on the tar roof pretty quick.

It weren't no time before everybody in town, even the men from over at the buggy factory, was on their way to the mill, doing whatever they could to help put the fire out. The fire didn't go out, though, and the weather didn't do nothing to help. The rain had stopped and there weren't nothing but wind and lightning and thunder.

Me and Little Carl and Aunt Clara had run down to the mill like everybody else, except she wouldn't let us get close to it. She was holding us back, watching the fire move through the place, window by window. A man in a uniform was trotting by us with a bucket. He looked at me and said, "Come on, boy, you need to help with this."

Before Aunt Clara could say or do anything, I took off running with the man. They put me in a bucket line, passing the water from the well pump to the fellows trying to put it out. The smoke from the burning cotton and bleach had all of us coughing and crying. I did my best to not spill any water when I passed the buckets.

I didn't know where Mama was. I knowed from what she had told me that she worked on the ground level and not in the upstairs part, but in the back, away from the doors. I kept looking for her, hoping that I would see her running by, but I never did. I just kept passing the bucket, passing the bucket. One line passed full buckets and the other sent the empty ones back. It was all we could do.

When the fire got so hot that a wall inside gave way and fell, they give up the bucket brigade. About the time they did, a sprinkle of rain started and fire on the outside started dying out. The smoke was still awful and it would be for the next three or four days. They got most of the fire out, but there was spots in there that would still flare up and burn on account of the oil that had soaked into the wood from the machines.

I walked back to the street, where Aunt Clara and Little Carl had been, hoping that Mama would be there with them, but she wasn't. Aunt Clara was crying and Little Carl was crying because she was.

Everybody I seen was crying and I knowed it didn't look good for nobody that was in there, especially the folks in the back. I heard somebody holler then and looked up and seen a bunch of folks staggering out of the smoke and into the rain toward us. Mama was one of them, staggering along and helping another woman who looked like she had hurt her leg pretty bad.

"We was in the back," Mama told us. "We was able to bust a little window open to where we could breathe, but it weren't big enough for us to crawl out through. We took turns breathing and when the wall fell, I thought we was dead sure enough, but we weren't.

"Mr. Oxley come busting in there to where we was and he started leading us out. He had us crawl most of the way, where we could breathe better. Something fell on Miss Burkeshaw's leg and hurt it, but we got her out anyhow."

Mr. Oxley was the onliest man amongst the women that had made it out of the fire. His shirt had been white, I reckon, but it was gray and black now and even reddish brown with blood on the front. He had took a bust in the mouth from something and his lips were both swoll up and bleeding. In that light, with the rain and the smoke and me with sweat running in my eyes from passing them buckets, I didn't recognize him at first.

It wasn't until that night when we got back to Uncle Henry's and ate supper and got in the bed that Little Carl said, "Old Socks done good."

"What are you talking about?"

"That was Old Socks that helped Mama and them other women out of the fire."

I cussed for the first time in my life. "Damn. It damn sure was, wasn't it?"

"Uh-huh."

I hadn't recognized him this time because of what he was wearing—that he was wearing anything, I reckon—and how scared I was about what was going on. "Mama said he was one of the bosses at the mill."

"You reckon Mama knows about him going at it with the neighbor woman?"

"I don't think so, but I sure ain't going to ask her."

"The devil started that fire," he said then.

"It was the lightning," I told him, "and not the devil." I didn't know what else to say. That talk about the devil always scared me. I wished he would quit talking about it. I just laid there and waited and after a long time, I heard him sleeping. The little rascal was bad about putting thoughts in my head and then going to sleep and leaving me to stay up and think about them.

I was still awake when Mama come to bed. She had been setting in the kitchen with Aunt Clara, crying about the fire and how she didn't have a job now on account of the place being burned. I waited till she had laid down and I asked her if she thought the devil had started the fire. She didn't say nothing — she just started crying. Finally she sighed and said, "I guess he did."

The next day Uncle Henry was gone to the buggy factory by the time we got up. Aunt Clara and Mama drunk coffee and fed me and Little Carl after we got our chores done. "We're going over to the mill," Aunt Clara said.

"You want us to play in the back yard till y'all get back?"

"No," she said, "I want you and Little Carl to come with us. May be something we can do to help out. You done right good yesterday, helping with them buckets."

I didn't want to go. The fire had been bad, but the things Little Carl said was worse and had me thinking about the devil being in on this. I didn't want to go. I was scared to see what the fire had done to that mill. I was scared that we might run into Old Socks and that this time he would recognize me and Little Carl. I thought about claiming that my stomach was hurting, but I knowed that was the kind of lie that would come back on you and you'd have a real belly-ache at a time you couldn't do nothing about it.

So off we went.

The mill was still smoking and one of the outside walls had fell in through the night. Looking at it made Mama cry. A few folks was walking into what was left of the building, looking and shaking their heads and poking with sticks at what was still left. I thought they was being foolish. I weren't getting nowhere close to it. You could see the pieces of machines that hadn't burned or melted still sticking up here and there. It was like the bones of the mill had been left when the mill died in the fire.

Folks standing around outside there told us that it had turned out three people had died in the fire. Two was women that worked upstairs in the back, right above where Mama worked downstairs. The other one was a colored fellow named Judge that had been the only colored man to work at the place. He cleaned the place up, usually waiting until it was closed to do it.

Yesterday Judge had come in early on account of the storm to see if a leak in the roof from the last winter showed back up. Judge done roofing work on the side and if he had been white, he'd have probably got rich off of it, he was that good.

They had found Judge pinned between a boiler and a loom. He had got scalded to death, they said, and the meat had cooked off his bones. One fellow went on and on about the smell of the burnt up man. It had smelled like a ham was burning, the man had said. That was a awful smell.

I felt sorry for him even if he was colored. The idea of being pinned there and getting cooked alive made me feel sick to my stomach. It scared me, too, and I couldn't quit thinking about it and sometimes it come back on me when I would try to go to sleep at night.

Mama and Aunt Clara walked around, talking to different folks, trying to find out what was likely to be done next. The folks that run the mill was from Pennsylvania and I remembered that was where that young man singer on the Fourth of July had been from, too. The folks from Pennsylvania was the Rokers and they had mills in Barnesville, Thomaston, Griffin and Macon. They had had them since after the war, one woman said.

There was a mix of crying and praying and fussing going on amongst the folks. Nobody knowed what the Rokers would do, whether they would rebuild or not and if they did, when they would do it. Some said that the Rokers hadn't made as much money with the Barnesville mill as they thought they would, so they probably were just as happy that it had burned.

While we were standing there, a bunch of colored folks walked up to the side of the property, looking on like we was, but further back. There was one big old fat colored woman right in the middle, looking like she was ready to squall if she got the chance. One of the women Mama was talking to said that was Judge's wife.

The coloreds didn't stay long. They turned around and started back across town to where they lived. A little colored baby was running and it tripped and fell and busted its head open on a crosstie next to the road. Its mama run and picked it up, trying to make it hush its squalling.

The women Mama was talking to just looked and then went back to talking while the colored folks went back to walking toward home. I wondered if that colored baby would have idiot spells like Little Carl did. I didn't know whether colored younguns got hurt like white younguns did or not.

Mama and Aunt Clara finally finished talking to the women there and we started walking toward the house.

"It don't look good," Mama said. "Not at all."

"Something will work out," Aunt Clara said to her, but it didn't sound much like she believed it either.

"The devil made the fire," Little Carl whispered to me as we walked behind the womenfolks. I was glad that he didn't say it loud enough for them to hear.

"I sure do wish you would quit saying that about the devil," I whispered back to him.

"I can quit saying it if you want me to."

I thought about that. Finally I told him, "Say what you need to say, Little Carl, but say it to me and don't bother Mama with it if you can help it."

I don't know whether he really heard me or not.

When Uncle Henry come home that night, he had heard that the mill wouldn't be reopening. The Rokers had decided they would do better to build a plant in Forsyth so that was where the new place would go. Mama cried and cried and Aunt Clara tried to make her feel better about it.

"You can find something else," Aunt Clara told her. "They always got jobs for folks that work good and you work real good."

Mama shook her head. "They may got jobs, but there is going to be a whole bunch of folks trying to get them jobs on account of losing the ones at that mill. If Mr. Oxley hadn't give me a chance, I wouldn't have found a job at all. He give me a chance and now he ain't got no job neither."

I hadn't thought about that, but Old Socks was out of work just like Mama was now that the mill had burned and wasn't going to be reopened. I wondered if there might be a way for the folks that worked there to start a mill of their own, but I didn't figure that would work since nobody had said it. I looked at Mama and thought how it seemed like there weren't no way for her to get ahead. Maybe the devil was after her after all.

Mama talked about leaving, but I knowed that she didn't want to really go. There weren't nowhere else for us to go except back to Caudell's and there weren't really nothing there. If we went back there, we might as well line up and jump down into that well.

Aunt Clara said, "If you give up now, you won't never know whether you could have made it or not."

Mama said, "I reckon you're right, Clara. I just feel like don't nothing ever work out for me."

Uncle Henry tried to get Mama on as a sweeper at the buggy factory, but with all the folks looking, sure enough, they didn't need to hire no woman that weren't even from Barnesville. They had done fired the two colored men that cleaned the place on Sundays so that they could hire some of the white folks that was out of work on account of the mill fire.

Come Sunday, we was setting in the back yard listening to Uncle Henry read to us out of a book about a fellow called the Virginian. It was a right good story and Uncle Henry done a good job of changing his voice different ways so it sounded like different folks was talking. There was a bad fellow by the name of Trampas and I knowed that sooner or later him and that Virginian fellow was going to have to fight it out.

Uncle Henry was reading and Little Carl weren't saying nothing and all of a sudden a fellow coughed. We all looked around and there stood Old Socks. "Henry?"

"Hey, Mr. Oxley," Uncle Henry said to him, like they knowed each other good.

They shook hands and Old Socks said, "I believe your sister-in-law is one of the women I helped out of the fire."

"That's right and we sure do appreciate it," Uncle Henry said. "I hate that the Rokers won't be opening the place back up."

"I do, too," Old Socks said, "but I have got another job and I wanted to talk to your sister-in-law to see if she might be interested in coming to work for me."

Uncle Henry grinned and hollered for Mama. As she was coming out, Old Socks looked at me and Little Carl and Little Carl must have been grinning because Old Socks got a real hateful look on his face.

When Mama got out there, Old Socks said, "I been hired to run that new store they just built across from the bank. I thought you might be interested in clerking there."

Mama said, "I sure am."

Him and her talked a little bit then, there in front of Uncle Henry and me and Little Carl. He told her that she ought to meet him the next morning at the back door of the place at eight o'clock and she said she would do that. He trotted off then and we all went inside and Mama told Aunt Clara about the new job while she made supper.

I got to thinking about Old Socks going at it with that neighbor woman. I figured if Old Socks was to try anything with Mama, she would put up a fight or she would come home and tell Uncle Henry one. Either way, I kept telling myself that it was going to be all right.

Of course, I knowed it wasn't. Mama didn't know nothing about clerking. It didn't sound like something you could just pick up neither.

I didn't even know if Mama could do figuring. If she could, I knowed
she probably hadn't done it since her and Daddy got together.

The clerking job worked out, though, because Old Socks had
Mama doing what they called "stocking and inventory" most of the
time. Mainly she was putting things on the shelves and moving things
around and telling Old Socks when they was running low on something.
For a minute, I thought Mama might have got lucky again.

By the end of July, Mama was coming home with things from
the dry-goods store most every night. It was usually little things like
some flour that the sack had busted on or a ham that had gone a little
green. It was nice because the job didn't pay as good as the mill job had
paid. Mama said that it weren't as hard as working at the mill had been
neither.

Come the middle part of August, they started talking about me
and Little Carl going to school. Aunt Clara took us down to the school
house and tried to get us registered for the fall, but the man down there
asked too many questions that Aunt Clara didn't know how to answer.
He said finally that Mama would have to bring us down there to do get
us in.

Another week or two went by and Mama finally got part of a day
off to where she could get us in school. I weren't interested in it at all,
but Little Carl was. He had got real good at listening to Aunt Clara
and Uncle Henry read stories and he would hold the books hisself
sometimes till it got to where he could figure out most of the words.
I weren't that interested and every time I tried to pick up the words, it
looked like marks and scratches and it didn't make no sense to me at
all. Aunt Clara said a good teacher would be able to teach me anyhow.

I went a long time without learning to read and write, but Aunt
Clara was right about finding a good teacher. I did finally, but it was a
good while later.

The day Mama took us down to the school, the man doing the
registering looked her over like he was in mind to buy her like she was a
cow or something. Me and Little Carl set quiet while he went through a

bunch of questions about us and her and Daddy. Mama didn't tell him that Daddy was dead, only that he weren't around anymore. The man acted like that was the kind of talk that would make him puke.

After a good hour, we was finally signed up and ready to go. The man told Mama that if we was any trouble, we would be put out and couldn't come back. Mama said we wouldn't be no trouble. I got to thinking right off that I needed to find out what that man meant by trouble and how quick I could get into it. I weren't keen on being a school boy.

Aunt Clara and Uncle Henry bought me and Little Carl some nice clothes to wear to school. I didn't much care for the new shirts. They was stiff and itched and felt like I had a piece of straw caught between my shoulder blades. The overalls was all right and the boots was extra nice. Little Carl got the same things I got, but a littler size, of course. He liked his clothes and, like I done said, he was real excited about the whole thing.

Me and Little Carl wound up in the same class. Since I couldn't read nor write nor do numbers, they put me and him both in the class with little younguns. Most of them was in the same boat we was, they couldn't read nor write nor nothing, but most of them was real little. The teacher was a nice woman named Mrs. Ellis. She told us that she was from DeKalb County and could speak and write French. I wondered what good that would do on account of most of us not even being that good at speaking and writing in American.

The first few days went by just fine. I done my best to do the work in class. Little Carl was ahead of me pretty quick, but he helped me whenever Mrs. Ellis wasn't looking. We done all right sitting together, but by the end of the week, she had figured out that our answers was always the same. "You may not allow your little brother to copy your work," she told me in front of the class. They all laughed and that made me mad.

"He ain't copying my work. I'm copying his."

They all laughed again and she asked me if I wanted to leave.

Well, that was about the best offer I had heard in a while, but I knowed that if I left, they would probably put both of us out of school and Mama would be mad about it. I said, "No, ma'am," and then I tried to keep my mouth shut. She moved me to another seat, away from Little Carl, and then neither one of us done very good on our work. I couldn't do it and he didn't like doing it without me.

Come the second week, they sent home a note to Mama that Aunt Clara had to read to her. It said that Mrs. Ellis thought there might be something wrong with her son and for her to come and meet with the man that had registered him again. It was right hard for Mama to get another hour off from the dry-goods store, but she did. She drug Little Carl down to the man's office and left me setting with Aunt Clara, cooking butter beans for supper.

She come storming back into the house a little while after that, madder than I had seen her since Daddy died. "They ain't talking about Little Carl! They are talking about you! They think you may be a moron."

Uncle Henry had got home by then and was setting at the kitchen table with us. He busted out laughing at what Mama said. She looked at him with her mouth all pinched tight and he shut it up.

"That teacher don't think you can do the work," she told me. "She thinks you ain't in your right mind. Now Little Carl here is going to town with it. He's done moved up to doing some of the work for the second grade. You're setting there, being stupid."

It hurt my feelings for Mama to say that, even if she was right. I didn't want nobody thinking I was stupid, but I sure didn't want to do anything that would make Mama feel bad.

"I'll try harder, Mama."

"You got to try a heap harder," Mama said. "You got to do as good as you can or they going to put you out and if they do that, you're going to work at the cotton field, do you hear me?"

"Yes, ma'am." I knowed how bad cotton field work was. It was bad enough when you were a youngun, being told to pick up the stray pieces and stick them in your bag and getting whipped if you didn't get enough.

To be a boy big enough to do the work meant that I would have to get up before the sun come up, find a ride to get to a cotton field, work all day in the hot sun, and then come home at night tired and nasty. The worst part of it was that in Barnesville, there weren't many white field hands. You would wind up working with colored folks all day long. I knowed I didn't want to do that, but I really didn't know whether I could get that school work down to where I could handle it.

Turned out, I didn't need to worry about it. Me and Little Carl didn't last long in school nor in Barnesville neither one.

Mama's busiest day at work was Saturday, when a whole lot of folks would come to the dry-goods store to buy what they needed. Like most of the businesses in Barnesville, they would close up for dinner at twelve o'clock and reopen at one. On the last Saturday in September, Mama was working with Mr. Oxley by herself. The other woman that worked there, a girl not no whole lot older than I was, went home sick that morning. When they locked the door for dinner, Mama and Mr. Oxley went into the store room in the back.

There was some big bags of flour and dry beans and rice back there and the next thing you know, Mama and Mr. Oxley was going at it on them bags. Since nobody else had a key to the store, they weren't worried about nobody coming in and catching them. They didn't realize that the little window in the back was open, though, and by the time they got done, a crowd of folks had gathered by window, listening and whispering and snickering.

When Mr. Oxley went back up front and turned the sign and opened the front door, the first one to come in was Mrs. Oxley, mad and ready to do damage. She pushed Old Socks right out of the way and went for Mama. Mama seen her and picked up a broom and swung it at the woman and cracked it across the side of her head.

The Fourth of July Queen went down like a sack of potatoes and Mama went out the door. She didn't stop until she got to the house and told Aunt Clara about it all while me and Little Carl listened from outside.

Chapter IV
SHAME

It was right clear that Mr. Oxley weren't in no position to cause nobody trouble, but his wife was. She weren't just the queen of the parade. It looked like she was the queen of Barnesville and she told everybody in town that this whore from Pike County had come and messed with her husband.

Uncle Henry was mad and sad and scared all rolled into one. He was mad at Mama and sad for us and scared for hisself. If them folks at the buggy factory got in their heads that he had brought Mama here, it wouldn't go good for him. He would get fired and likely never work in Barnesville again. He'd have to move somewhere else and start over.

"What little I had saved up, I spent on you and them boys," I heard him telling Mama. "We ain't got much of nothing to start over with."

Mama cried, but she cried for her own self, not for Uncle Henry. Aunt Clara didn't cry at all. I think she was just pure plain mad with Mama. She started to say something two or three times, but never did finish any of it. Folks get like that when they're mad with kinfolks sometimes.

Aunt Clara brought us supper in our room that night. Mama took hers to eat outside. Little Carl didn't even ask if he could go with her. Mama was by herself for that little while.

On Sunday morning, me and Little Carl got up to find Mama had done packed all of our stuff and put it in Mr. Caudell's wheelbarrow.

Uncle Henry didn't come out to see us. I was glad he didn't because I felt so bad about what had happened, what Mama had done, and I didn't want him to look at us. We just needed to get on away from them. It was like we had brought a sickness with us and the best thing we could do now was to go before we made them any sicker.

Aunt Clara didn't say much to Mama, but she hugged and kissed on me and Little Carl like it was the saddest day of her life. I didn't know what to say so I kept my mouth shut. Little Carl told her that we loved her, which I thought was right nice. She said that after a while, maybe at Christmas, she would borrow a mule and ride out to see us.

I didn't much figure that was going to happen and it didn't.

Mama was dressed a might nicer now than when we had got there in May. Her hair looked nice and her face was all healed and her clothes were store-bought and pretty. I couldn't let her push that wheelbarrow, looking as nice as she did, so I pushed it. It felt like I had pushed it all the way to Pike County before we stopped to eat what she had brought for us. There was biscuits and a glass jar of pickled peaches. That was something that Aunt Clara would give us special once a week and when I saw that jar, I knowed Mama had took the whole thing when Aunt Clara wasn't looking. We ate the pickled peaches and biscuits under a pecan tree just inside the county line.

Mama pushed the wheelbarrow the next little ways and I kept looking, hoping we might catch a ride with nice folks like we had when we had gone to Barnesville. I reckon it was a off day because there sure weren't many folks traveling.

Two come by us, headed the other way. One was a sour looking old woman on a horse and the other was a man pushing a wheelbarrow hisself, but his had a sick pig on it that he said he was taking to a root doctor to look at.

Mama got tired after a while and I started pushing again. "I don't know how much longer I can keep pushing at all," she said. "I don't know."

A breeze blowed through, but it was a hot, dusty one and left you hotter and dirtier than you had been before. We weren't making too good a time getting back to Caudell's.

"You reckon Gladys is still there?"

"I don't know where she could have gone," Mama said.

All this time, Little Carl was quiet, not talking about the road or the trees or telling a story about rabbits that wore clothes and talked, just quiet. I looked at him and seen that his idiot spells was back. He was stumbling along beside Mama like the moron that Mrs. Ellis thought I was.

Finally a wagon come up behind us, but it was full of colored folks. The big fat colored woman riding beside the young buck driving hollered, "Miss, do you need a ride?"

I expected Mama to say something smart back to her, but Mama stopped and said, "I would rightly appreciate that."

"Jackson, jump down and help these white folks," the woman said.

A skinny colored man set our stuff up on the wagon and then set me and Little Carl up there. He pulled a big wood block down off the back so Mama could step up and climb onto the back of the wagon herself. Once she was sitting down with us, the man put the block on the wagon again and took his place on the seat.

"I seen you before," the woman said.

Mama didn't say nothing back to that. I think she was scared that woman had been in the crowd outside the dry goods store, but there weren't no way that would have happened. There weren't no colored folks in that part of Barnesville.

"You was at the mill after the fire."

"Yes, I was," Mama told her. "I worked there. I liked to have got killed in the fire, like to have burned up in it."

"My Judge, he did get burnt up."

"I'm sorry," Mama said to the woman, like she meant it. "I heard tell he was a good worker and could do roofing work, too."

The fat woman said, "Judge learned roofing from his daddy. It didn't make no sense to me, but he knowed how to lay shingles to where the water wouldn't get up under them. He could do a flat roof to where it didn't leak neither, not even around the pipes and along the edges. Judge had talked about going to Chicago, but we never done it."

It sure was sad, listening to that colored woman talk about the man that had burned up in the fire. I wondered if she had heard what we had heard about him cooking. She probably had. She quit talking and looked like she was about to bust out crying. She just turned and looked at the road the rest of the way. Like I said, it was right sad.

We rode on, setting up there on the back of that wagon pretty as you please. Nothing else was said about Judge or the fire or roofing. When we got to the corner where Mr. Caudell lived, Mama told the woman and they stopped and we got off. Mama thanked them and the woman said she believed in helping people, which I thought was right nice, even if she was colored.

I pushed the wheelbarrow up the road, looking at Mr. Caudell's house, wondering if he would come out and holler at us. I was pushing and walking and looking and seen Gladys through the window.

At first, I didn't think it was her. I thought it had to be Mrs. Caudell, but I knowed better. It was Gladys. I stopped and stared and I knowed she was looking at us. I waved a little bit. Mama and Little Carl didn't see her at first and then they did. In a minute she was running out the door towards us.

"Why are y'all back? What happened?"

Mama hugged her and cried. They went and set on the steps of Mr. Caudell's house. I left the wheelbarrow setting at the road and me and Little Carl went and set with them. Mama told her some of what had happened, how the mill job had been so good and then the fire and then just that she worked at a dry-goods store but that didn't work out so good.

"Where's the baby at, Gladys?" Little Carl asked her.

"It died," Gladys said. She didn't look real sad about it, more like she was disappointed. I remembered how it didn't even have a name that I knowed and I wondered how they buried a baby without a name.

"What happened to it?"

"It got sick in June. It had the whooping cough, I guess. It cried and it coughed so much that it couldn't eat and when it did, it threw up what it did eat. It got puny and couldn't keep nothing down. I tried giving it milk and bread and water, but didn't nothing work. It died."

"What did you do with it?" Little Carl asked her.

I was scared she was going to answer him and I didn't want to hear it. She didn't say nothing, though.

Mama asked her, "What you doing up here at Mr. Caudell's?"

"This is where I stay now."

"Uh-huh," Mama said and looked around at the place.

"I asked him for a job," Gladys said.

"He give you one?"

"He got me to come up here and keep house for him."

"What happened to his wife?"

"She didn't much care for me being the housekeeper," Gladys said. "She has people in Alabama and they come to see her and after they all talked about me, she got her things and went home with them to Alabama."

Mama looked at her.

"She ain't coming back," Gladys said. "I'm running this house now."

Mama said, "We're going to need a place to stay. Did he get somebody else to work on shares where we was?"

"He tried, but it was too late in the year when—when Daddy left and y'all went to Aunt Clara's."

"You reckon he would let us stay there and try to work it for what's left?"

"I can ask him when he gets back. He's gone to Griffin and won't likely be back until night."

"Can we eat?" Little Carl asked her, not being bashful about it at all.

"Caudell has a good bit of groceries right now," Gladys said. "I don't reckon he'd miss a little bit."

We followed her inside and she took us to the kitchen. We set down and she fed us. Mr. Caudell — she just called him "Caudell" — eat pretty good, it seemed to me, especially when I considered how Daddy had had such a hard time getting him to give us a line of credit at the store in town.

Mama spent the whole time looking around at everything and saying how nice it all was. She liked the house and she liked the yard and she liked all the things Caudell had. She sent me and Little Carl to the outhouse and it was as nice as Uncle Henry's had been, even though he didn't keep no powder in it for the smell.

We finished eating and Mama said, "It's too dark for us to go all the way down to the house."

"You can't stay here, Mama."

Mama just looked at her.

"Take you a lantern with you in case it gets too dark."

Mama said, "Give us something to eat tomorrow until we see Caudell."

Gladys went into the kitchen closet and come out with a cloth sack and handed it to Mama.

Mama took the bag and started to leave. We followed her. She said, "We'll come back up here in the morning, before he leaves for the field, and I'll talk to him then."

Gladys shook her head and said, "Mama, I'll tell Caudell when he gets home tonight. If he wants to talk to you, he'll come and see you. Just stay at the house." They had acted different since the baby was born, but this was even different from that. It was Gladys acting like a grown woman is what it was. I didn't much care for it and I knowed Mama didn't.

We got to the house before dark. Mama lit the lantern and we went in. Nothing much had changed except all of the baby's things were gone. I took Little Carl to the outhouse so we could do our business. I wished we had a lantern to take with us on account of there might be a snake in there. The moon was out and there was a little bit of light from it. I was glad when we got out of there and headed back for the house.

I was starting for the house but Little Carl just stopped, looking out towards the field. "Where's Jip?"

I swear, I hadn't give Jip a thought. "I guess he run off, Little Carl."

He didn't say nothing back to that. I felt bad about the dog. Caudell had come and got his animals, but he probably didn't pay no attention to Jip, if he even seen him.

"Jip's probably off in the woods somewhere," I said.

Little Carl didn't say nothing else about the dog. We walked on to the house.

Mama had brought in the things from the wheelbarrow. Me and Little Carl went on to bed and she come in there in a little bit and got in the bed with us.

When I heard Little Carl snoring, I whispered, "Mama?"

"What is it, son?"

I set up and said, "What are we going to do?"

Mama pulled herself up and leaned towards me. "We ain't got much choice, son. We're going to sharecrop right here."

"What if Caudell don't let us stay?"

"You're still a little boy, ain't you, son?"

I didn't say nothing back.

"Mr. Caudell is going to do whatever your sister asks him to do. He's that kind of a man. He might cuss and he might fuss, but Caudell will do what he has to do to keep Gladys happy."

I thought about that. Daddy didn't seem to care what Mama wanted nor us neither. I spoke before I could stop myself. "Why didn't you marry a man like that?"

She hit me in the mouth. "I done what I had to do. Now Gladys is doing what she has to do."

"I didn't mean nothing."

"Your sister is lucky your Daddy didn't do worse than he done. I know what he could do when the mood hit him. She don't."

She flopped back on the bed, mad at what I had said and more mad at the thoughts it was making her have. I laid down slow there with Little Carl between us. I wished I had kept my mouth shut, that I hadn't said that to her. She felt bad enough, I reckoned.

When I woke up the next morning, I was by myself. I went through the house, looking for them. I went out the back door finally and found them pulling up sweet potatoes from the garden. It was only thing we had planted back in the spring that the weeds hadn't killed. Most of the potatoes was skinny little things. It was going to take most of them to make one good meal for the three of us, if it come to depending on them.

Mama saw me and said, "Caudell ought to be here in a little while."

I looked at them on their knees in the dirt, digging for the little orange roots and piling them up as they found them. There weren't no way we could make it two days on what there was on the place. And nothing we could raise from here till winter was going to make enough for Mr. Caudell to front us the credit to keep us on.

"Go in the barn and see if you can find them rabbit boxes your daddy built and go set them in the woods."

It was too early for rabbit, but I done what Mama told me. There was two boxes out there that was in good shape and a third one that needed a new trip. I brought the two good ones out and walked across the field to the woods. The boxes was made from scrap and would fall apart pretty easy so I toted them careful. When I got into the woods a little ways, I set one of them down and propped the trip door. I didn't have nothing to put in it for bait so I would have to go back and get something and come back. I didn't know what we would have that we could use. If there was some rotten vegetables, it might draw a rabbit, but I figured we'd be eating all the vegetables we could find, ripe or rotten.

I took the other trap further back and seen that I was on the path toward where that well was, that well where we had put Daddy.

I laid the trap down, didn't even think to set it, and trotted as fast as I could back to the house. "I ain't got nothing to bait them with," I told Mama.

She looked up from the digging and said, "Maybe we can get Caudell to give us something."

Maybe we could, but what little I remembered about Mr. Caudell didn't make me think it was likely.

Little Carl had quit digging. He was just setting there and I knowed that he was slipping back into the idiot spells. Mama wasn't paying him no attention and I wondered if she even seen how he was. She pulled a sweet potato out that had a long skinny root hanging off of it. She broke that off and put it in the pile with the rest of them.

I walked back in the house and set down on the blanket that the baby used to lay on. I remembered how it would giggle when Daddy weren't around and it would well up and cry if he got too close to it. I wished it was still around.

I got to studying about the baby then like I hadn't done before. I wondered who its daddy was. There weren't many folks that it could have been on account of us not going nowhere without Daddy.

I heard Mr. Caudell come up out front, riding his wagon. He hollered and Mama went out. I come around the house to listen myself to what was being said. I don't know what he had said at first, but Mama was telling him that she was back and wanted to work the farm for him.

"Your husband and me worked pretty good together. I hate that he run off and left you, but that ain't none of my problem. If I let you stay here till next planting season, I expect you to keep the place up and not cause me no trouble. You think you can do that?"

"I can," Mama told him, "but I want to work for you next year."

"Woman can't do what needs to be done. I know you're in a tight spot, but that ain't none of my problem," he told her again. "You stay till the spring and I'll have somebody else come in and plant this one."

She walked closer to him where he set on his buggy. I walked up closer so I would hear better, but she was saying something to him too low for me to pick up.

"I don't know about that," Mr. Caudell said. He acted like he wanted to get down off the wagon, but then he looked over at me and set where he was. "I don't reckon your girl would care much for that, would she?"

I couldn't hear what Mama said back. I just seen the way Mr. Caudell looked and knowed that he wanted to get away. He said, "I told you you can stay the winter. Do what you can by next planting season and I'll think about it. Right now, you got to get through the winter." Then he hyahed his mule and was gone.

I didn't like that. There weren't no way we could make it there through the winter. We didn't have nothing canned, didn't have no money, didn't have nothing. I reckoned that Mama thought she could get Gladys to keep giving us food and things, but I didn't think that was going to work. Mr. Caudell would sure see what was going on and put Gladys out and us, too.

"We can't do it," I said. "What we going to eat? We ain't got nothing."

Mama slapped me. "We ain't got no choice is what we got."

She walked into the house and I stood there in the yard.

Right then I believe I could have walked off from the place and never looked back. I didn't, but maybe I should have. Maybe everybody would have been better off. I was just so mad I didn't know what to do and I thought I had to stay on account of Little Carl. Dern his time, the little fellow was like a chain tied around my leg, keeping me from going anywhere too fast and from going anywhere at all most of the time.

I was mad at Mama about what had happened in Barnesville. Aunt Clara and Uncle Henry had been so good to us, took such good care of us. As much as I hated school, I would have gone every day if we could have stayed there and things had stayed like they was. I wondered how in the world we was going to make it.

We didn't eat nothing the rest of the day. Me and Little Carl spent the afternoon digging through the sweet potatoes, looking to see if we could find anything else, but all we came up with was a few more pieces of little twisted roots. I broke up some of the littlest pieces and took them out to put them in the rabbit boxes.

"I'll go with you," Little Carl said when I told them where I was going.

"No," I said, "you need to stay here with Mama. I won't be gone long. When I come back, you can tell me a story about that rabbit."

Little Carl didn't say nothing back to that. He knowed I was just putting him off. He didn't like it, but I couldn't help that. Right then, I couldn't have him coming with me.

I took the pieces of them sweet potatoes to the woods and fumbled around till I found the first one, the one that was close to the field. I put some of the sweet potato along the edge of it and a lot more back, close to the trip.

The other rabbit box was further back, on the path to the well. I started towards it, looking everywhere for anything we might be able to eat. Daddy had talked about poke salad, but I didn't know what that looked like.

I finally found that other rabbit box. I got down beside and put the pieces of sweet potato into it. I really didn't expect to catch no rabbits. It was too early for them, and there was plenty else for rabbits to eat. I couldn't help thinking the rabbits was better off than we was right then.

If I had had a rifle or a shotgun, I could have hunted, I reckon, but I didn't. I might have killed squirrels or birds or possums or anything. I didn't have no gun, though. Daddy had sold the only one he ever had. His daddy had give it to him. He sold it back when we lived on that other place, sold it one year when things was going pretty good, I thought. I didn't know what he had spent the money he got for it on.

When I finished baiting the rabbit box, something caught my eye off up ahead and I knowed it was that piece of tin that covered the well where Daddy was. I set the trip on the box and stood back up and started to turn around. Then I don't know what possessed me, but I started towards that tin.

My dead Daddy was down in that well and had been for a while now. Didn't nobody but us and Mr. Caudell seem to notice that he was gone. It weren't that odd for a fellow like Daddy to just go missing. You would hear folks say, "He's gone to Texas." That meant he had run off and didn't nobody know where he was. Anybody that knowed us wouldn't have blamed Daddy for running off, not that anybody knowed us.

I crept up to the piece of tin and looked at it. The rocks covered up most of it, but enough of it shined through that it had caught my eye from a good way off. I walked over to it, thinking about the trouble we was in and how even now I was glad he was dead.

"You ought not been so mean to us," I said like Daddy could hear me. "You didn't have the devil in you. You was the devil. You was. You didn't have to kick us all the time. You done what you done to Little Carl and you done what you done to Gladys. That baby probably died—" I stopped right there because I didn't want to go putting more on the man than he had really earned. But he had sure earned a lot.

"Hurting mama like you did, you ought not to have done that. She makes mistakes like anybody does, like you made. She didn't need to be beat like you done her." I was crying and mad and hungry all at the same time. "I hope you in hell. I hope you burn and burn."

I had never much believed in hell or heaven, but like grown folks, I didn't mind talking like I did when the situation come up.

I wiped my nose on my sleeve and stared down at what we had made Daddy's grave. I reached in my pocket and got the piece of sweet potato root still in there and put it in my mouth. It was nasty and hard and not sweet at all. I chewed on it and sucked the juice. I heard a noise.

I looked up and seen somebody off a ways. I tilted my head and squeezed my eyes and seen that it was a colored boy about Little Carl's size. "What you doing out here?" I hollered at him.

"I ain't doing nothing," the boy hollered back at me.

"Why you out here?"

"My daddy told me to come out here. He's got a…" The boy didn't finish what he had started to say. He just stopped and changed it. "What *you* doing out here?"

"Setting a rabbit box," I told him. "And you better leave it alone. I come back out here and there ain't no rabbit, I'm going to come looking for you."

"I ain't messing with your rabbit box. We got rabbits. We don't need to mess with yours."

"Where you get a rabbit?"

"My granddaddy. He keeps them in a pen behind his house. He raises rabbits and goats, too."

That made me even more mad. Here I was so hungry I was eating sweet potato root and this colored boy had rabbits and goats and no telling what else to eat.

"You better leave my rabbit box alone," I said. I started backing up real slow, wanting to move on out from there and get back to the house. I spit a piece of the chewed up root. I turned around and started slow.

The boy didn't say nothing right off but then he hollered "Hey!"

I turned back around.

"Who was you talking to?"

"What?"

"Who was you talking to in that well?"

You might say I come undone at that point. I didn't know what in the world to say back to him. I knowed I was in trouble. I knowed that.

He asked me again, "Who was you talking to in that well?"

"I ain't talking to nobody."

"You was. You was talking to somebody in that well."

"No, I weren't."

He didn't say nothing back to that and I knowed he didn't believe it.

I said the only thing I could think of. "I was praying."

"That weren't no praying. You got somebody in that well."

I started to just run, to go back to the house and hope didn't nothing come of it. You couldn't tell. Most of the time, the law wouldn't get involved with something that colored folks brought up. I couldn't be sure of that, though. It worried me.

The boy hollered again. He said, "They dead?"

"Ain't nobody in that well."

"I'm going to look when you're gone." He said it like it was some kind of joke he was cracking. I didn't care for that at all.

"You better stay out from over here. There ain't nobody in that well."

"Then you go on. And after you gone, I'm going to look." I could see he was grinning.

I swear I didn't know what to do. I was mad at myself on account of coming back here to the well instead of going back home when I had the chance. "What you doing in these woods anyway? This belongs to Mr. Caudell."

"I don't know no Mr. Caudell. Mr. Louis Jenks owns these woods."

He might have been right. I knowed that the well was supposed to be on Mr. Caudell's land, but over where he was, I didn't know. "This well is on Mr. Caudell's property and you better stay off of it."

He didn't say nothing back and I knowed all I was doing was making him want to look in that well even more than he already did.

I walked back over toward the well. I didn't get too close to it, but I got closer than I had been. I set down on the ground and looked. I could see him a little better now. He was older than I thought at first, probably old as I was, but littler.

"You tell me who is really in that well and I'll go on and leave you alone," he said. "You can go home and I won't look."

"Ain't nobody in the well."

He set down on a stump and looked at me. I waited as long as I could. It was when he grinned at me again and I could see his teeth against that black face that I finally give in.

"It's my daddy," I told him.

"Your daddy?"

"It's my daddy in the well."

"Why is he in the well?"

"Him and my mama got in a fight and she killed him and I drug him here and put him down the well."

"Your mama killed your daddy?"

"Uh-huh."

We just set there for a while then. Finally I asked him, "You want to see him?"

"You said he was in the well."

"He is, but you can see him."

He didn't answer. I went to the well and pulled the rock off and then moved the tin and then moved the planks.

I leaned and said, "There he is, right there. You can see his head if you look just right."

He started walking over towards me and I backed away from the well. When he got close enough, I grabbed him. I was used to wrestling with Little Carl to try to make him do whatever Mama told him to do that he didn't want to do. I reckon I thought that boy would be like wrestling with Little Carl, but it weren't.

He pulled aloose from me and took off. I run after him, figuring he was going to outrun me pretty good on account of the head start that he had. He didn't though, he stopped a little ways ahead and turned back around. "All right, white boy, I ain't going to bother your well, but you leave me alone and go back to your house."

We stood there for a while then, just looking at each other. If I had of been him, I would have run all the way back to where the grown folks was, but I didn't know whether he would think to do that.

"You heard what I said. You get on back to your house. I'll leave your well alone."

"Don't tell me what to do."

He tilted his head down. I had seen Daddy do that right before he took to whipping on one of us. It weren't but a second and he come charging at me. I kicked at him when he got close enough, but I missed anything worth kicking and he knocked me back in the dirt and vines.

He was strong to be so little, but he didn't weigh enough to hold me down for long. He was hitting me in the head and I took to rolling and throwed him off of me. I jumped up and kicked him in the neck and he hollered. I kicked him again in the face and seen blood bust out of his nose.

"Uncle! Uncle!"

I hadn't never heard nobody say that before so I didn't know he was trying to give up. I wouldn't have stopped nohow. "I ain't your uncle!" I kicked him a few more times till he quit hollering and quit fighting back. I dragged him by the legs back over to the well and slid him down into it. He was kind of messed up, but he knowed what I was doing and he said, "Please don't, white boy, please don't."

He slid head first down into the well.

I didn't hear him hit, but I heard him moan after he did. I put the planks back over the hole as quick as I could and then the tin and then most of the rocks, but I was in a hurry and didn't put them all back. I figured I would do that when I checked the rabbit box the next day, but I forgot about it.

I was tired and scared. It would have been bad if that boy had gone back and started telling folks there was a dead man in a well back in the woods. Somebody might have come out there to look. There weren't no telling what would have happened.

When I got close to the house, I seen that first rabbit box, the one close to the edge of the woods, had been tripped. I figured I hadn't set it right and that the trip had come loose. I started to reset it and derned if a little rabbit didn't come hobbling out. There was something wrong with it. One of its hind legs was about half not there. If it had been in good shape, I never would have caught it. With that messed up leg, I was able to grab it pretty quick.

I popped it, broke its neck and toted it by that good hind leg back to the house. It had turned out to be a pretty good day after all.

Mama said it weren't big enough to fry, but that we could sure make rabbit stew out of it. I skinned it and gutted it and she boiled it till it fell apart. It was good and we ate on that rabbit stew for two days.

That was the last rabbit I got in one of them boxes, too. I went out there to check on them again the next day. Little Carl come with me so I didn't go nowhere close to that well, scared he might hear that boy moaning down in there. I didn't need that.

We went without for a day. We had well water and Mama scared up some greens that she said was poke salad, but they was so bitter, couldn't none of us eat them.

"It don't taste right," Little Carl said to her.

She was trying to eat it, but she weren't making much headway neither. She finally reached over and got the bowls setting in front of us and took them and poured all that mess out the back door. "I reckon I ought to have hung on to your daddy a little while longer," she said. "Might have a use for him yet."

She didn't say what she meant and I didn't ask.

Mama walked back to Caudell's the next day. I thought she must have asked Gladys for their scraps because it sure seemed like she come home with a bag of the nearest next to nothing I had ever seen. I swear I thought Gladys had give her the garbage bag from Caudell's house.

Thinking back on it now, I can see it might have really happened that way. Mama would have gone through the trash while Gladys watched her out the window, neither one of them saying nothing to the other one. The way they was acting I wouldn't have put it past them. Both of them was stubborn.

Mama took what she had got at Caudell's and made stew with it, but it was a right sorry stew. There weren't no meat to go in it so by the third day it weren't nothing but water and a greasy spot.

"I reckon I'll walk back up to Caudell's," she said late in the day. She made to look up at the sky.

"It's late, Mama. Do you want me to go?"

"Ain't no need for us both going," she said, "but I believe it would do your sister good to see you and Little Carl both."

I didn't know about that on account of how late it already was. "We could both go, but there ain't no telling how long it would take with Little Carl going. I could go and be back a lot sooner by myself."

She didn't seem like she heard what I said. "Your sister don't want to help her old Mama none, but she won't turn you boys out. I reckon she still got a soft spot in her hard heart for you two. You go and take your little brother with you and y'all be careful."

Little Carl was having his idiot spells right regular again by then and I figured we'd have to stop a few times on account of that. I was expecting to spend a good bit of the daylight that was left standing by the road while he looked off at nothing with his mouth hung open.

He didn't, though. He was good the whole way to Caudell's. He didn't have a single spell. We come to that corner and I seen Gladys standing in the back yard taking clothes down off the line. Soon as she seen us, she come running towards us. "Hey! Hey, Little Carl!"

My little brother grinned and run up to her and they hugged like I don't know what.

"I sure am glad to see y'all."

"We hungry," Little Carl said like it was something he had been told to say as soon as we got there.

"Y'all need to come on in and eat." We followed her into Caudell's house and out to the kitchen. She had a pot of beans going on the stove. Gladys went into Caudell's ice box and got out what they had left from the supper the night before. There was some smoke links that had been fried. They was mighty good. She had some biscuits, too, and give them to us with jelly somebody had traded to Caudell when peaches had come in the summer before.

We eat it up. We hadn't had nothing good to eat in a few days and we couldn't help eating like pigs now that we did. While we eat, Gladys finished bringing in the clothes. She come back in and walked around that kitchen like it was her place and I reckon it pretty much was. At first, it had looked to me like Mr. Caudell had took her in and made her work for him, but now I seen that he might have took her in, but she wasn't just working for him. It looked like she was running the house.

"I reckon Mama sent y'all down here for groceries."

"Uh-huh," I said back to her. It hit me that I didn't know that I might not be able to walk all the way back to the house with my belly as full as it was, particular if she give me a big sack to haul.

Gladys rummaged around and come out with a flour sack that had a few things in it. "Tell her that's got to do her a week. Caudell didn't sign on to feed that old heifer, too."

I looked in the bag and it was even sorrier than what she had come home with the other day. "Can't you give us some more, Gladys?"

"You done eat a good helping of Caudell's grub. What do you want now?" She knowed full well what we wanted and why we wanted it. I was hoping she would just give us something we could make stretch for a while where we would have something to eat. "You done eat and there's you something to take home."

"I just hate to go back to Mama with that little amount."

"Mama could of done a whole lot better. Don't go feeling sorry for her. She don't deserve it."

I didn't say nothing back right then. I knowed Mama had brought a lot of things on herself. She was bad about doing things that Daddy had told her not to do, making him mad and starting trouble. She had messed up pretty bad in Barnesville. Still she was our mama and we needed to help her. I knowed that much. "Please give us some more food to take home for Mama, Gladys."

She shook her head at me like I was a fool.

I looked in that sorry sack again at the mess she was sending home to Mama. Before I could figure out what to say to try to get her to give us more, there was a big crumping noise in the front room. Me and Gladys went running in there and seen Little Carl standing there over a doo-dad that had been hung on the wall.

It was a thing made to look like Jesus hanging on the cross. Little Carl must have tried to take it down, but the thing was heavier than it looked and it had fell to the floor and busted. Jesus had got knocked slap off the cross and was laying face down over next to the wall with his arms spread out like he was jumping into a pond.

"Oh, hell. Oh, hell," Gladys groaned. "Caudell is going to have a fit when he sees this."

I picked it up. That Jesus was right heavy and must have been made out of iron. I tried to put him back on his cross, but the nails that had held his feet and his right hand had broke off. The only one still working was the one that held that other arm. When I tried to get Jesus to stick on the cross, he would swing on the left hand like he was wanting to come down off that cross and play.

There was a pop sound. Gladys had slapped Little Carl so hard her handprint was across his mouth. He was about to bust out squawling. "You done busted Caudell's little Jesus. He's going to take that out on me when he gets home tonight."

Little Carl started crying and I put my arms around him. "You know he didn't mean to do it."

"Mean to do it? Don't matter to Caudell no more than it mattered to Daddy what you meant to do. What gets done is what gets your butt whipped." She looked down at the broke Jesus and shook her head. "Y'all need to get on before Caudell comes home."

We headed back for the kitchen. I picked up that cloth sack and said, "This ain't enough food, Gladys." I swear you could see her near about bust when I said that.

She snatched that sack out of my hand and went around the kitchen and shoved a world of things into and then handed it to me and said, "Now, y'all take it and get out of here. Tell her I don't want her nor y'all to never come back down here. I ain't going to rob the man to feed her."

I didn't say nothing back to that. That sack was full of things that Gladys had grabbed just to get rid of us. I wondered which would make

Caudell more mad, that broke Jesus or them missing groceries.

Little Carl cried off and on all the way home. It was starting to get dark when we left Caudell's and it was plumb dark when we got to our house. Mama had laid down and gone to sleep, but she got up when we come in. She snatched the bag out of my hand and busted out laughing when she seen how much was in it. She dumped it out on the table and some of it fell into the floor.

"I knowed she would be good to you boys. I knowed she couldn't be mean to y'all."

"She said not to come back, Mama, not you nor us neither. She said she weren't giving us nothing else."

"She takes after her daddy, a lot of talk," Mama said. "She won't turn her back on y'all."

"Little Carl broke Caudell's Jesus and she slapped him, Mama, slapped him across the mouth right hard."

Me telling it made Little Carl remember the whole thing and start crying all over again. "Don't cry, honey," Mama told him. "You ain't the first to break somebody's play pretty and you won't be the last."

She got a fire going in the stove and started cooking. I told her again that this needed to last us a long time. She wouldn't have it, though, and cooked near about everything in that bag that night. Me and Little Carl was too full to eat so we went on to bed. Mama thought we was doing it to be ornery and so she stayed up and eat her fill of what we had brought home.

The next morning we got up and there weren't much left of the things we had brought home so we set down and eat a little of it. When Mama got up, she eat the last biscuit.

I told her I was going to check the rabbit boxes and she said to take Little Carl. I was glad to do that because that way I had a reason not to go to that well. We walked across the field and kicked at clods as we went. The field hadn't got its second plowing nor been planted so it was in rough shape. I was thinking how rough it was going to be if we did have to try to plant the whole place come next spring.

Little Carl was having a good morning and with food in his belly, he was trotting along ahead of me, picking up clumps here and yonder and throwing them just to watch them bust to pieces when they hit the ground.

We got to the first rabbit box and it was empty. When we started deeper into the woods. Little Carl said, "What you scared about?"

"I ain't scared of nothing."

"You dreamed about something last night and whatever it was scared you."

"I don't remember," I told him. I was telling him the truth. I didn't remember. He was probably right that I had dreamed something bad, but I didn't remember it.

We walked on to the other rabbit box. It was still set and it didn't look like nothing had even been close to it. I thought about moving it, but I knowed moving it closer to the field wouldn't be good and moving it further into the woods meant going towards that well.

I left it where it set and me and Little Carl headed back for the house. "I wish we lived close to a creek. If we lived close to a creek, we could catch fish to eat."

"How? We ain't got no fishing poles nor no bait and I reckon we would need both."

"I'd just get in the water and grab them fish with my hands."

Since we hadn't never lived close to no creek, I didn't know whether you could just up and catch a fish with your hands or not. It was that kind of thing that made me wish Daddy hadn't kicked Little Carl in the head. There ain't no telling what that little fellow might have thought up if he had been right.

He stopped walking and cocked his head. I thought he was starting a spell, but he was listening to something.

"What?" I asked him.

"Listen." I stopped and listened. It was a rattle, right loud, coming from towards the house. We took off running, wondering what in the world was making such a racket.

The closer we got to the house, the louder the noise got.

When we finally got in sight of the house, we seen it was a car, setting in front of our house, two wheels on the road and two in our yard. A fellow wearing a fancy outfit made out of leather was setting on the front seat of the thing, messing with handles and pushing peddles while the automobile jumped around like it was having a fit.

We had seen a few cars back in Barnesville in the Fourth of July parade. Uncle Henry had said they were called funny names with them letters they had tried to teach me in school, but we hadn't never seen one at our house. Me and Little Carl come running up to it and got within a arm's length when that driver hollered, "Get away!"

We backed up but I don't reckon we done it fast enough, cause the man hollered again.

Little Carl stopped dead still, deciding then to have one of his idiot spells. Before the man could holler a third time, I said, "Mister, he don't mean nothing. He ain't right."

That man looked down from that car at us like we was something that turned his stomach. He looked away from us and toward the house and I looked that way, too. There was Mama, standing there at the door, talking to two men. The pop-pop-popping motor was making way too much noise for me to hear anything being said.

Whatever they was saying had Mama right upset. I watched and tried to figure out what was going on. I seen that one man was in a brown uniform, wearing a badge and reckoned he was the sheriff. The other one was a big fellow about half bald-headed with his hands poked way down in his pockets and a cigarette setting between his lips.

Mama was shaking her head. The half bald fellow was saying something and then the sheriff was talking to Mama. She looked like she was crying. The sheriff looked to have finished what he was saying and him and the other man walked back to the car. I caught hold of Little Carl's arm and snatched and pulled him toward where Mama was standing with her hands over her face.

The man driving the car had to make it go forwards and backwards over and over before he got it turned around and headed back up the road. The sheriff and the other man jumped in it. The sheriff set on the front seat next to the driver and that other man pulled hisself into the back seat. The car pop-pop-popped and spewed and then shook itself on up the road toward town.

As soon as it was quiet, I asked Mama, "Who was that?"

"The sheriff and some fellow named Jenks. Jenks owns the land that backs up to this place and he's lost a little colored boy and has the sheriff out looking for him."

It was the boy I throwed down the well that they was looking for. I said, "Why they come here looking?"

"They just looking everywhere, asking everybody what they seen," she said. "That Jenks man said the boy's family has been on his place nigh on fifty years. Mr. Caudell must have told them your daddy had run off. They was asking all about when was the last time I had seen him. They acted like he had something to do with that boy." She shook her head and busted out crying again. "Lord, I thought we had got away from the man, but damned if he ain't coming back on us anyhow."

I looked over at Little Carl, who was still feeble with his own idiot spell. It bothered me awful that Mama was getting upset all on account of the boy I had put down the well. I reckoned I had really been the one to cause the sheriff to be looking at us, not daddy. I got to thinking about it and that was when I throwed up. There weren't much in my stomach, but what there was all come shooting out.

Mama said, "What's the matter with you?"

"I guess I'm scared, Mama."

She was mad. "You think I ain't? You know what they would do to me. You seen what they do."

"What did you tell them?"

"Nothing," she said. "I didn't tell them a damned thing. They asked a lot of questions about your daddy and I got to crying and they thought it was because I was crying over him."

"Then you ain't got nothing to be scared of," I told her even though I knowed better. I knowed she was scared to death because I was.

"They're looking for that boy but they might find your daddy."

I felt like I was going to throw up again, but I didn't.

That was when Little Carl said, "We could go live somewhere else." The little fellow had come to hisself and was thinking as best as he could. "We could go somewhere and call ourselves something different and say our daddy died from the flu."

Mama turned on him. "Boy, where we going to get the money to do that? You think your sweet Aunt Clara is going to help me?"

"Mr. Caudell's got money."

Mama drawed back to slap him, but stopped herself. "Caudell's done stuck his nose into this mess against us. Your sister's got him working against me."

"He's got money," Little Carl said.

I swear I was tempted to slap him then. But I got to thinking about what he was saying. That was the thing about Little Carl when he weren't having a idiot spell, he could come up with things that made you think.

Mama just walked off. She went and set down on the steps in front of the house. Little Carl set down beside her and put his head against her leg. There weren't room for me to sit down with them, so I walked around to the back of the house.

The field that Daddy never got to plant that year was setting idle as far as you could see. There was patches of weeds here and there, but nothing we could eat, I didn't reckon. I thought again about poke salad and wished I knowed what it looked like so I could try to find some of it. I thought about not finding it. I thought about not finding it and us starving to death.

I thought about what Little Carl had said. Caudell had money. If we had just a little bit of his money, we could go somewhere else and set up housekeeping there. I knowed it was crazy to think about that because Caudell weren't going to give us nothing. Gladys weren't likely to help us out none neither.

I wondered if we could get Aunt Clara to send us a little money, but I knowed that I didn't know how to send her no letter and even if I did, I didn't know if she would do it behind Uncle Henry's back. I knowed he wouldn't send us anything. Mama had near about messed him up in Barnesville.

I went and dug some more where them sweet potatoes had been planted. I didn't find no whole lot, a handful of fat roots, mostly broke off from big pieces and rotting on the ends. I took them to the well and drawed water and washed them off and then went inside, started a fire and got a pot of water going on the stove. I put the sweet potato pieces into the water when it got to boiling. I took the sack Gladys had sent home with us and shook it over the pot. The salt and flour and couple of dried beans in the bottom of the sack went down into that pot.

"What you doing?" Mama said. She had come in while I was busy with the cooking, I reckon.

I looked up and said, "I thought I would try to make sweet potato soup. Am I doing right?"

She didn't say nothing, but got a look on her face that was sadder than it had been already. She went and got a spoon and started stirring. Finally she said, "Go outside with Little Carl and I'll finish this."

I done like she said. Little Carl was still setting there on the front steps. I set down next to him. He looked around at me. "We could live somewhere else and not have these troubles."

"I know." But I didn't believe it. Troubles latch onto you and don't let go easy. I knowed we didn't have no way of leaving neither. I wished Little Carl would have said something different, told one of his talking rabbit stories, but he didn't. All he done was say something else about the money that Caudell had.

We eat the soup just before dark. Boiling them roots made them softer but not so soft that you could bite them apart. You could chew and chew and still have a mouthful of it.

When we got done, I told Mama I was going to go check the rabbit boxes on account of the rabbits running at night. She knowed better than that but she let me go. Her and Little Carl went on to bed.

I went toward the woods a little ways then cut over and got on the road. There was a little bit of a moon that night so I could see pretty good. Now I reckon the dark had scared me before, but that night, it didn't have nothing on me. I trotted along, knowing what I was going to do and hurrying to do it.

When I got to Caudell's, I seen light coming from inside. Closer up, I seen that Gladys was setting at the table, eating with Caudell. He was a good sized old fellow, bigger than Daddy had been in all directions. He was shoveling it in and Gladys was picking over hers like she weren't hungry at all.

I went up to the back door and tapped on it. A dog woke up in the backyard and come charging at me, howling a bark and woo-woo-wooing to beat the band. The door snatched open and Caudell was standing there with a pistol in his hand. I about messed my pants up.

"What you want?"

"I want to talk to Gladys."

"It's my brother, Caudell," Gladys said from behind him.

"I know who it is. Little thief done come to haul off more of my groceries after I been good to his Mama and him."

"I ain't come after nothing but to talk to Gladys."

The dog was still cutting his mean howling barks. "Hush, dog." The big man turned back, grabbed Gladys by the arm and pushed her toward me. "Talk to the boy, but if I catch you giving him anything, I'll bust you again."

He went back in. The dog started behind him but he kicked it and it went back out. When he was setting back down at the table, I said real low, "We need to go somewhere else, Gladys. Me and Mama and Little Carl can't stay here."

"You sure can't. Caudell found that broke Jesus and he whipped my butt and then he come through the kitchen and seen what I had give y'all and whipped me again and then he..." She didn't finish, just looked mad at me and finally said, "Well, he's done made up his mind that y'all got to go. He was going to come out tomorrow to tell your Mama to get gone by the end of the week."

I whispered, "What did he tell the sheriff about the colored boy?"

Gladys just looked at me, mad. "He didn't know nothing about that boy. Caudell says the Jenks man is always bringing the law on somebody. The colored can't keep up with their younguns. That one probably wondered off and fell-"

She looked at me. I don't know how much of my face she could really see in the dim light on that porch, but she seen enough.

She asked me, "What happened to that boy?"

"He come up on me in the woods. He seen me at the well and he wanted to come and look in it."

Gladys turned her head, chewing on the inside of her mouth as she done it. "Damn."

"He was going to look in after I left, Gladys, so I caught him and throwed him down in there."

"Is he dead?"

"By now he is, I reckon."

Gladys looked at me, mad but thinking. "That sheriff goes to looking in them woods for that boy, he'll look in that well and then we're done."

"That's why we got to leave."

"Didn't nobody look for Daddy," she said. I was seeing her better now, even though it was dark. She was right bruised up. Caudell had give her a bad whipping. "Let me think on it."

I started to say something else, but there weren't nothing I could say that would matter.

"Send him on his way, Gladys!" Caudell hollered from inside.

"You need to get on back home," she said loud enough for Caudell to hear her, then low, "I'll come out there tomorrow while he's in the field."

I done what she said. It was dark and it scared me walking home on that road. I was seeing things and people in the shadows where I knowed there weren't really nothing. I ain't never been one to be scared of ghosts and things that you know ain't really there, but that night, I wasn't sure what was there and what weren't.

She did show up the next day. It was way later in the morning than I expected, but I know I was just so scared, I couldn't track the time no way. Gladys finally come trotting up on one of the mules we used to have. "He knowed something was up," she said to me as soon as we met up at the edge of the yard. "He hung around and hung around and I didn't think he was ever going to leave."

She had rode one of Caudell's mules and she tied it over by the porch where it could eat the weeds by the house. I said, "If we could get maybe twenty or thirty dollars and a mule with a wagon, we could get gone. Mama talked one time about living in Newnan when she was little. If we went there, we might be able to get a place in town and she could work in the mill and I'm big enough I could work in the mill, too, if I got the chance."

"You ain't got no better sense than Little Carl if you think Caudell's going to give up anything to y'all right now and he sure as the devil ain't going to give away no mules and a wagon."

I felt the devil in me just then and said what I was thinking. "I know he ain't going to give it. I didn't say nothing about him giving it. It's what we got to have, though."

Gladys looked at me hard. To this day, I wonder what she seen. Was it me or was it the devil? Or was it something else?

Mama seen it was Gladys that had come to see us, but she didn't come speak to her. I couldn't blame her. It weren't like they was mama and daughter right now. It was more like they was two snakes that might bite one another if they had the chance. Little Carl didn't hold back though. He run out and hugged Gladys like he didn't remember at all the broke Jesus nor the trouble that had caused.

Me and her set down out back, far enough from the house that I knowed Mama couldn't hear us and where we could see if Caudell was to come riding up. "I been thinking about the whole thing," Gladys said. "I don't know that any of this will work. It didn't work when y'all went to Barnesville on account of Mama being a whore. You might get to Newnan and her be a whore all over again."

"Mama just don't pick men good, Gladys. You know that."

Gladys shook her head. "Men sure do mess things up for women, that's for damned sure."

"You going to come with us?"

Gladys said, "I don't know. I got a little problem here myself and I don't know whether I want it or not."

I thought she meant Caudell beating on her, but it turned out that weren't it.

Little Carl said, "When we going to leave?"

"You hush," she said to him. "You got to be quiet about this like you ain't never been quiet in your life. You tell folks about this and there ain't no telling what might happen to us. Sure as they world, they would hang Mama. It could be worse than that. They might hang all of us."

"We brought the devil home with us," Little Carl said then. "We brought him home with us so he could help us."

"Hush, Little Carl."

Gladys said, "If y'all hang around here, it's going to get hot for all of us."

"It wouldn't take no whole lot for us to get by a little while. If we had enough money to do us a week or two, we could get by. We could go somewhere else."

Gladys spit and looked around to make sure there weren't nobody listening. "Caudell has some money set aside for his payment to the bank. If y'all come to the house Thursday night after midnight, I can slip that money to you and you can head for Newnan. It would be better if you could take a wagon, but there ain't no way to get the mules out without him knowing it. That money ought to get you a place and a start when you get to Newnan.

"Caudell's going to beat the hell out of me for that. He may throw me out, but I doubt that he will. He sure likes his pleasures and I don't much figure he'll give it up easy."

"If he throws you out, you can come to Newnan with us," I said.

"I appreciate it, but I don't reckon me and Mama get along good enough for that. Y'all just need to get out of here while you can."

"How long you reckon it's going to take us to walk to Newnan?"

"A day or two. When you get to Haralson, you ought to find you a place to stay. I imagine there's a boarding house or two that would let you stay a night or two if you need to. Lay low. The more folks sees you, the more folks might say something to the sheriff about you."

I hadn't thought that part through. I had figured on us catching a ride part of the way. That wouldn't be no good idea, though. Getting out of Pike County wouldn't be enough. We'd have to get out of the state to get away from the law and even then we might still get caught if we had bad luck. Bad luck was the one thing that it looked like we always had plenty of.

But at least Gladys was going to help us. Maybe our luck would change. That was the first time me and Little Carl had set and talked to our sister since we left for Barnesville and it was nice. Gladys talked a while, telling us things we either already knew or didn't really understand no how. Not a time did she say a thing about that baby. I wondered if it hurt her so much to lose it that she didn't want to talk about it. Right then I got to missing the little thing, wondering if it had wound up in the well, too. If it had, Gladys weren't letting on.

We seen Mama looking at us out the window. Gladys said, "She don't never change, does she?"

"What you mean?"

"She ought to have come and seen me, not sent you slipping back around."

"Gladys, she didn't send me."

"Boy, she's so sneaky, you don't even know she sent you."

"She didn't," I told her. Mama hadn't sent me. She hadn't.

Gladys shook her head and then she said real serious, "I ain't never coming to look for you. If you get big enough one day to come back here on your own, come and see me. If he ain't died, bring Little Carl with you."

Little Carl grinned, happy to be included, I reckon.

Gladys got up and went and got the mule and walked him to the edge of the road. "You come after midnight Thursday night," she said again. "There won't be no talking nor hugging nor nothing. Just take what I hand you and go. You make sure Mama knows that y'all need to get on as far away from here as you can. The longer you hang around here, well. The longer you hang around, the more likely we'll all hang."

Little Carl trotted after Gladys on the mule till they was out of sight and then he turned around and come slow back to the house. Poor little fellow sure did love Gladys.

After she was gone, I went in the house and talked to Mama. I told her most of what I had in mind. I halfway figured she would slap me and not go along with none of it. She didn't though. She just nodded her head and then went to the bedroom and laid down.

It weren't but a couple days until Thursday, but I worried about the trick we was pulling to the point that I didn't set down much of the whole time. I walked the field and pulled different greens that looked like they might be good to eat and finally found one that I thought was probably poke salad. We cooked it down and put some wild onions in with it. It weren't much, but it was better than water soup. I come on a dead turtle when I went to check the rabbit box on Wednesday. I opened it up and we eat good that night and the next day.

Chapter V
WIDOW

⌐≣⊨

Thursday finally came and we set out late in the evening. I didn't have no idea about checking no clock to see when it was midnight. I just knowed by the moon when the night was about half over and figured that would do good enough. Mama was letting me tell her what to do and Little Carl was fumbling along with me most of the way. I got Mama to load up our clothes into sacks we could carry easy. Yeah, I wished we had mules to ride, but that weren't the way it was.

Leaving the house there for the last time scared me to death. It weren't the only place we had ever lived, but it was probably the best one, not counting when we stayed with Aunt Clara and Uncle Henry. Little Carl didn't remember living nowhere else, but I did. This one hadn't been so bad. There weren't many leaks in the roof and the walls didn't whistle when the wind blowed. For a sharecropper's place, it had been pretty good, I figured.

We walked in the moonlight down the road toward Caudell's place. I bet I seen more rabbits jumping into the road and across the field that night than I ever seen in my life. It hurt, thinking how them dern things was running around playing when I had needed them to get in my rabbit box so bad.

That made me remember. I had left them rabbit boxes set. Now, if a rabbit was to wander into one and get trapped, it would just stay in there till it starved to death and then wouldn't nobody likely find it till it was bones. It would be a shame for rabbit to go to waste like that.

When we finally come to Caudell's, Little Carl and Mama stopped and stood and waited for what I was going to do. I walked real quiet up to the back door and, sure enough, that blamed dog come barking at me. The back door opened and Gladys stepped out. She throwed a hunk of meat to that dog and he snatched it and run off into the dark to eat.

She give me a canvas bag. "Go," she said. "Go just as fast as y'all can. The money is in there and, here," she handed me another sack, a good sized paper sack, "this here has some food for y'all to eat on the way."

I started to say something, but Gladys shook her head and shooed me away. If that dog barking had woke Caudell up, he'd be out here in a minute, wanting to know what was going on. I figured he was likely to shoot if he seen his money was gone.

"Go," she said.

I took the bag with the money in it and stuck it into my overalls' pocket to where I wouldn't have to worry about toting it nor losing it. The sack with the food in it was welcome and I hung on to it so I could be sure we all had something to eat when the sun come up.

We walked all night long and as morning started to come, we was all moving pretty slow. Mama hadn't said nothing since we left the house. Little Carl was quiet, and I was right surprised at him walking so far without telling me he needed to stop and rest or having one of his spells.

There was enough light to see a little bit by then. We was coming into Zebulon, walking past the courthouse where we had seen the man hung back last spring. We walked by the bank and the Methodist Church and was on our way to the road that would take us most of the way to Newnan.

"We need to stop for a while," Mama said finally. But we were near about out of Zebulon by then and I wanted to get as far as we could before we stopped. The sun was up and there was a good many folks in the street, going here and yonder, and I didn't want none of them to pay no attention to us. Mama didn't put up no fuss and neither did Little Carl. It was like I was the onliest one doing the thinking.

When we were a ways past Zebulon, we come on a empty shack by the road. The door was standing open. "If you want to, we can stop and rest here a while," I told Mama.

"I'm dying from all this walking," she said. "If I could just set down for a while, it would help my poor feet."

The door was standing open, but the steps was busted up pretty bad, and we had to climb up into the little house. There weren't nothing to it but two rooms. The little bit of furniture that had been in it was busted to pieces and scattered. We set down in the floor, but it weren't a minute before Little Carl was snoring. Mama stretched out, too, and I knowed I wouldn't last long myself.

I pushed that old door to and laid myself out across in front of it and put my sack of clothes under my head for a pillow. I figured that way, nobody could slip up on us. If they pushed that door, it would wake me up.

The next thing I knowed, I was sound asleep, too. I don't know how long I was out. I woke up a good while later when I felt Mama fumbling around.

"What you doing?" I asked.

"Where's that money at?"

"I got it."

"Open it up," Mama said. "I been scared she might have slipped us a sack of washers. We ought to have counted it before we left."

I didn't think Gladys would do that to me and Little Carl, though I knowed she might very well cheat Mama if she could. I set up in the floor of the little shack. It was late enough that the sun was pretty bright outside and it was poking all through the holes in the walls. I figured we weren't going to make it to Haralson by dark if it was as late as I thought it was.

I reached inside my overalls and pulled out the canvas bag. I shook it and then pulled the draw string that was holding it shut. I turned it up, expecting silver dollars to tumble out. I was wrong.

It weren't silver dollars at all. It was *gold*. They had eagles on them and I remembered Daddy calling them "twenty dollar gold pieces" when he would get to fussing about what somebody else had that he ought to have. Daddy had talked a lot about gold and money for a fellow that didn't never have none.

Mama counted it up and said there was seventeen of them and she tried to do the figuring on how much money that was, but she couldn't do it too easy. She stacked the money up over and over and finally said that she seen it to be more than three hundred dollars.

Little Carl reached to pick up a stack of them, thinking they was play pretties, I reckon. Mama slapped his hand away and said, "Uh-uh. I'm going to hang on to this. Your sister has done took right good care of us for a change."

It scared me to know we had that much money. I don't know how come it to scare me. You would think that having money after not never having none before would be a good feeling for a fellow, but it weren't. All I felt was scared and it weren't on account of knowing that money weren't ours. It was knowing that it was three hundred dollars, more money than I had ever heard tell of anybody really having. You could do anything with that much money. That was a scary feeling.

I didn't trust Mama to tote it, but I didn't know what to say to her about it. She took up that canvas bag and went to put the gold pieces back into it, but there was something stuck in the bottom of the bag. She reached in and jiggled and come out with a pair of scissors.

Mama dropped them to the floor. It had to look a second time before I realized them was Mama's scissors that she had killed Daddy with. There was blood still on them, dried to a brownish color like rust.

"That little bitch," Mama said then. She grabbed up the money then and stuck it all in that sack and then stopped. She looked at them scissors laying there and finally grabbed them, too, and stuck them back into the bag. She went to stick in inside her dress but then she handed it back to me. "You hold on to this and don't let nobody, not nobody, get it."

I thought Gladys had put them scissors in there so we would have something to fight with if anybody tried to get that money away from us. "I wish she had put a pistol in there where we could shoot some of them rabbits," I said. "Ain't no telling how many we'll see before we get to Newnan."

Mama shook her head. "We ain't going to Newnan."

"Why not? I thought we was going to work in the mill."

"Damn that girl," Mama said. "Damn her." She went over and peeped out the door like she thought there might be somebody out there, but there weren't. "We ain't going to Newnan. We're going to Orchard Hill."

Little Carl sat up. "We going to pick peaches?"

Mama didn't pay him no attention. She said, "We don't know nobody there and don't nobody know us."

I didn't understand what she was talking about. It didn't make no sense to go somewhere that we wouldn't know nobody. Orchard Hill was where Mr. Caudell had took corn, but that was about all I knowed about it.

By then we was hitting the road again, going back the way we had come at least a little ways. I was right glad that we weren't walking as far. I have to admit that I didn't like Mama changing our plans, but I sure liked the idea of cutting our trip shorter by six or eight hours of walking.

We walked back into Zebulon in time to come up on a wedding letting out at the Methodist Church. There sure was a heap of folks there and we was already amongst them before I thought about how we were supposed to be careful about who seen us.

Finally the two that got hitched come out of the church. The boy was wearing a gray suit, but the girl was dressed up like I don't know what in a white dress that drug the ground. Folks hollered at them and waved and they waved back and grinned real big.

About that time, a colored fellow driving a buggy pulled up and stopped right in front of the church and I expected sure as the world for somebody to whip him for messing up that wedding, but they didn't.

The two of them just grinned and climbed up in the buggy like they was expecting it to pick them up. The colored fellow driving didn't look around or nothing. He just hayahed the horses and off they went with folks hollering and running along behind him like they wanted to bring them back.

One old lady was just standing there crying and crying while some more was patting her and saying how it was going to be all right.

We walked on down the road right amongst folks heading home after the wedding. I could tell something was working in Little Carl's head. "Why was that woman crying?"

Mama kept on walking. "She's probably that gal's mama and she knows what she's in for. You can't tell a young girl nothing. Not a thing."

We was moving along pretty good when we finally turned onto the road to Orchard Hill. I half expected Mama to break into a trot we was walking so fast. Little Carl dropped the sack with the crackers and cheese in it and we had to stop to help him pick it up.

When the man in the wagon spoke to us, it scared me because my mind was somewheres else, as they say. I'd been thinking about Mama and Daddy ever since the wedding and wondering if they got married in a church, but I knowed they didn't.

"You folks need a ride?"

I looked up and here sits this fellow on the buckboard. He's the kind Daddy would have said looked like he hadn't never done a day's work in his life. He's looking down at us with a grin that showed his teeth.

"We headed to Orchard Hill," Mama told him.

"I'm going up to the Experiment Station by Griffin," he said. "Y'all welcome to ride with me. I could use the company."

Much as I was scared of the fellow, my feet was hurting to beat the band and I was probably up on the back of the wagon before he finished offering us the ride.

Mama helped Little Carl get up there with me. Then she got into the seat next to the man. That grin of his got bigger and I wished I didn't see all them teeth. Nobody I knowed had *that* many teeth.

I pulled myself and Little Carl up to where we could lean back on the buckboard seats and we could hear most of what was being said. "You got people in Orchard Hill?"

"My brother and his family," Mama lied. "We headed up to see them. Be the first time since my husband passed."

I couldn't see him, but I knowed that man's grin didn't get no smaller. "I'm sure sorry to hear that. I lost my wife about six years ago and I know it can be hard. Hard."

"It is," Mama said. "Judge was a good man and didn't never hurt nobody and it was just such a shame that he fell off that house he was working on."

"He was a carpenter?"

"Roofing," Mama said. "One of the best around. We was doing right good till he died." It worried me that Mama was coming up with this business about Daddy that weren't true nor even close to it.

The man was quiet for a bit. "I knew of a colored man named Judge. He died in the mill fire and I hear tell *he* was a roofer."

I thought Mama was caught, but she weren't. She was too sly. "The colored Judge had worked for my husband at one time," she said. "That's where he took his name from. My husband was Judge, but they called that one 'Nigger Judge' on account of him being a good roofer, though he weren't as good as my husband."

The man quit talking a good while. I thought maybe Mama's story hadn't made no sense and the man thought he'd done picked up some crazy folks. Finally he said, "I work for the University."

"That's nice," Mama said. She didn't know what that was no more than I did.

"It's the school up by Griffin," he said. "Well, the University is over at Athens. The part of it I work with is the Experiment Station in Griffin."

"Uh-huh." I was glad Mama didn't come up with no story about her husband Judge building no University somewhere. She laid low on that one. Finally she said, "What you do up there?"

"I teach."

"Ooooh!" Mama said like it was the best thing she had ever heard tell of. Me, I thought of that Miss Ellis and wondered why in the world a man would want to sit in a room with a bunch of younguns all day. I reckoned that maybe when they got bigger, it took a man just to be able to make them all stay inside all day.

The man grinned again. "That young fellow who just got married was one of my students last year. His father died from the flu, and the boy asked me if I would be his best man."

Mama didn't say nothing because she didn't understand what the fellow was talking about. Of course, I didn't know neither, but I was a youngun.

We rode on a little while longer and come to a rickety wooden bridge on the road. The man stopped his wagon and got down. He walked over to the bridge and started across it, stepping hard on every board to make sure the thing would still hold up enough to support his wagon. I watched him, thinking that if it had been Daddy driving, we'd have rode halfway across and dropped down into a spot where the wood had rotted and spent the rest of the day cussing and fussing and trying to get the dern wagon on across.

The fellow sure seemed to know what he was doing. He tested the bridge, come back and drove that wagon right careful across. When he got to the other side, he stopped again. "I believe I could stretch my legs for a while, if you all don't mind."

"We sure don't mind," Mama said. She didn't no more look at me and Little Carl than the man in the moon. Her and this fellow was walking off down the creek that run under that bridge. They went plumb out of sight down the creek and I didn't need to follow to know what was going on. I reckoned Mama was paying for that ride after all.

Me and Little Carl opened up the sack and split a cheese biscuit while we set there. My legs had been stretched enough and I was pretty sure Little Carl's had, too. We set there a while and he dozed off. I reckon I did, too, because we was a ways on up the road when I woke up and seen that the fellow and Mama was on the seat and the wagon was moving past a good-sized cotton field.

We had rode a good ways when we come upon brick posts on either side of the road and a sign on one of them. The fellow read it out loud, "Welcome to Spalding County." Then he said, "We are getting close."

Mama said, "Uh-huh. It will sure be good to be around kin people again."

"Did you say it was your brother and sister-in-law or your sister and brother-in-law you was going to see in Orchard Hill?"

"My brother and his wife is who we are going to stay with," Mama said, "but I call her 'Sister' a good bit so I might not have been clear about it."

"Uh-huh," the fellow said.

Little Carl was setting up and looking around right then, looking at the farms that we was going by. Some of them looked to be doing pretty good. I got to wondering if three hundred dollars was enough to buy a little place we could farm ourselves. I didn't know and really didn't know how to go about finding out. Then I thought about the fellow we was riding with. "Hey, fellow," I said to him. "You reckon we could buy us a place for three hundred dollars?"

"That ain't nothing to be asking!" Mama hollered at me. She looked over at the fellow and said, "I am sorry about that. The little one ain't right and the bigger one ain't much better."

"Oh, that's all right," the fellow said.

We rode just a little while longer before Mama said, "The boy's question is a right good one. Could we get us a place here for three hundred dollars?"

"I don't know," the fellow said. "Might want to talk to your brother about that."

Mama started to say something and stopped. I bet she was about to say, "Brother?" and I am right glad she caught herself.

"Look a yonder!"

There was a great big silo up ahead. Me and Little Carl stood up on the back of that wagon, looking ahead at it and wondering at the sight of the thing. "We're getting into Orchard Hill," the fellow said. "Tell me where your brother is and I'll drop y'all off at his door."

"No," Mama told him. "My brother has some right funny ideas, right old-fashioned ideas about how widow women is supposed to act. You just let us off at that silo and we'll walk the rest of the way."

The fellow said, "I respect that. I don't reckon I would want my sister riding with a strange man either." Nor walking the creek line, neither, I thought to myself, but I kept my mouth shut.

"I appreciate your kindness," Mama said to him.

"If you ever need me, you can telephone the Experiment Station up in Griffin and the operator will get the message to me."

"I don't reckon I will be using no telephone," Mama said. "I don't much believe in them."

The fellow pulled his wagon over at the silo and we climbed down. Mama whispered to me, "You still got that canvas bag?" I checked my pocket and nodded to her. She looked up and smiled to the fellow and said, "We are much obliged for your kindness. You have saved a widow woman and two orphans from having to walk the rest of the day."

The fellow grinned again like he had at first. "If you ever come up to Experiment…"

"We'll be right here in Orchard Hill," Mama told him.

"And if I come through again, would your brother mind if I stopped by to visit with you and your boys?"

"I tell you what," Mama said. "If you think you might be coming through, send me a letter to the Orchard Hill Post Office."

His grin got bigger. "I believe I will do that." Then he stopped. "What name would I put on it?"

Mama didn't have a answer ready for that and had to think, which I could see troubled the fellow a good bit. "The Widow Judge," she said.

"I thought Judge was your husband's given name."

"It was," she said, "but that's how folks knows me around here." She all but dared him to say anything else.

We watched as the wagon drove on down the road and then took to walking again. There was a sign for a store and a arrow pointing so we went in that direction. Turned out that there was four different stores — three on one side of the street and a big feed store across from them. There was a little café at the end of the street. Right behind that feed store was railroad tracks. There was a little house across from there.

There was a few folks here and there, but not as many as we had seen in Barnesville. Mama stopped in front of a store that didn't sell nothing but clothes. They had things hung up in the window and Mama was looking and I wondered if we would have any of that money left if she was to take a liking to the clothes in that window.

There was a little sign in the window that said "Room for Rent." We went inside the store and seen a man standing behind the counter with a newspaper in his hand. We was a rough looking bunch, I reckon, but that man looked up from his paper at us like he smelled something to turn his stomach. I didn't much like it.

We walked around the store a little bit. The fellow put his newspaper down and watched us with his nose all turned up. "We don't sell on credit."

Mama didn't say nothing to that only kept looking around at the shelves and shelves of clothes. Me and Little Carl walked around with her, but I kept looking at the man looking at us. Mama picked up a shirt and you would have thought she had pulled a knife on the man the way he acted. He come running over there and snatched it out of her hand.

He said, "Are you buying? We allow for looking, but not for handling."

Mama said, "Show the man our money."

"Mama, we need to go," I told her.

She drawed back like she was going to hit me but she stopped and said, "It's all right, honey. This here is a honest man."

I reached into my overalls and got the bag out and reached in it and pulled out one of them gold pieces. The man looked at that double eagle and then back up at us. I was glad I had just pulled out the one.

"You want to buy some clothes with that?"

"We was interested in that room you got for rent."

That fellow looked at the bag that I was holding and then at that double eagle. "I reckon I might be able to rent it to you, but I'm going to need a deposit."

Mama looked at him and he seen she didn't know what he was talking about.

"You got to leave money with me in case you tear up the room. I can't have you tearing up the room and then running off."

"Where is the room at?" I asked him, thinking he was going to put us in the back of that store behind that little curtain he had strung up behind where he set.

"Upstairs," the fellow said.

"How much you want to let us stay there?"

"Be a dollar a week," the fellow said. "There's stairs in the storage room back there, but y'all need to come and go by the stairs on the back of the place."

"Then why you got stairs inside?" I asked him. As soon as I said it, I knowed I had said too much.

That fellow turned on me and opened his mouth and I expected him to lay into me about smarting off. He stopped before he said anything and looked me up and down. "The back stairs are better," he said. Then he smiled and looked back to Mama.

She smiled back at him and I knowed we was sunk.

"You keep that gold piece there and tell me when it's used up and I'll find you another one."

He seemed to like that idea and took the money and put it in his pocket. "Come on, then." He motioned for us and we followed him behind the cloth curtain that separated the main part of the store and to a set of stairs that looked right rickety even in the dim light.

We followed him up the steps to a room that had the biggest bed I had ever seen, a window that looked out onto the street and a slop jar made to fit up under a chair like it was built for it.

"I had figured on renting the room out for a week at a time to traveling fellows," the man said. "You know what I'm talking about: the men that come through selling this and that. We get them right often. Bill Summerlin and his wife runs a boarding house, but it's a little pricey. Mrs. Summerlin is a right good cook, but not as good as her prices are."

Mama didn't say nothing back to that. I kind of wondered about these Summerlin folks and their boarding house. If they had a place to stay *and* fed you, it sounded like worth learning a little more about. We didn't, though, on account of Mama and the clothing store man.

He went over and opened the back door and showed us the stairs he wanted us to use. There was a outhouse a little past the back steps too. He showed us the well between this building and the next one and said we could use it for water.

"I believe you folks will like it here just fine."

"I believe we will," Mama told him.

"If you need anything else, come and see me. My name is Jimmy Gordon."

"I'm the Widow Judge," Mama told him. I reckon it was easier doing that than coming up with something new. "My husband died of the flu. He was a teacher in the spearmint place in Griffin." I knowed the fellow didn't believe her. Leastways, I knowed that if he had a brain in his head he didn't believe her.

He looked funny at us and then acted more polite than it made sense to. "Well, if y'all need anything before closing time, let me know. I don't live far and I come in early and I stay late so I'm near about always here if you need anything."

"We'll be fine," Mama told him. "I'll be looking for a job and I reckon we'll start looking for us a house right after that. We sure appreciate you being so nice to a poor widow-woman and her younguns. The Lord's going to bless you for that." I wondered where she got that last part from because I hadn't never heard nothing like that pass Mama's lips before.

Jimmy Gordon with a twenty-dollar gold piece in his pocket didn't say nothing. He just smiled.

Mama smiled at him again. He looked at Little Carl and then at me and then he left.

We laid down on the bed as soon as that man left the room and Mama started telling tales about what we was going to do that made that one about rabbits wearing clothes and talking sound right sensible. "We can get us a car and go somewhere and buy us a house."

It didn't matter that didn't none of us knowed how to drive a car nor how much a car cost nor how to go about buying a house. It didn't matter. It was talking rabbits wearing clothes. It was pretty to listen to but it didn't mean nothing. I went to sleep with her still talking.

I woke up the next morning and Mama was gone. I run my hand inside my overalls, checking for the moneybag. Sure enough, it was gone and I knowed Mama had took it. I hopped up and got my boots on and run down them back steps. I left Little Carl asleep and didn't even think about him when I took off. I was down them steps and looking when I heard Mama calling my name.

"What you in a hurry for?"

"What did you do with that bag?"

"I got it." She was walking back from the outhouse, not in no hurry at all. I wondered if she had done already lost the money. She went back up the steps to our room and I followed her. Little Carl was still asleep.

Mama bought us new clothes that day. We got shirts and britches nicer than what Uncle Henry and Aunt Clara had bought us. Mama bought herself a pretty red outfit that Jimmy Gordon said was brand new and the fanciest thing any store in Georgia outside of Atlanta would be selling.

After we got the clothes, we walked to a eating place that was down from the clothing store. We went in there and there was folks setting and eating and didn't none of them turn around to look at us on account of the new clothes.

We set down to a table and a woman come over and asked us what we wanted to eat. I said I wanted some streak-o-lean. The woman said she would see if they had some, but would bacon be all right if they didn't. I said it would. We went back and forth with her like that till she was satisfied that they would have what we wanted or we would want what they had. She brung out glasses of tea for us and we drank them down and had another one.

The food sure was good, but it cost us near two dollars and I knowed we wouldn't be able to afford to eat like that all the time. There was a general store that we went to and got things to keep in our room and eat. I was glad we didn't have no cooking stove in there because I believe Mama would have got more groceries than we could have toted. As it was, we went home with near three dollars worth of things. We was living high on the hog, as they say. Even though I weren't but a youngun, I could still tell that that couldn't last long. It didn't.

The next morning, Mama got up and put on some of her new clothes and said she was going to find a job. I looked at her all dressed up and knowed there weren't no job I knowed of where a woman dressed so nice could do it.

"You and Little Carl need to stay here in the room till I get home."

"I figured me and him would go see if we could get jobs, too." I was lying. I was planning on following her so that if anybody tried to get that money, I could keep them from doing it.

"No," she said. "You two stay here. You'll be done got in trouble in town. You ain't used to being in town and you need to just stay here till I get back."

"You might better leave that money bag here with us."

She didn't say nothing back to that. She just fluffed that outfit she was wearing and headed out the door. Mama weren't worried about us getting in trouble. I think what she really wanted was to look more like a young woman than a old mama and that was really why she didn't want us out and about with her.

Me and Little Carl set and looked out the window for a while, but there weren't much going on. From our window there, we could look down on the main street of Orchard Hill and watch the farmers coming in for the things they needed and the fellows that run the stores coming and going and the like. There was a few women walking around, but very few. The few that there was was either rough dressed farm women come to help tote things or dressed nice like they was going to fancy doings.

Weren't none of them women dressed as fancy as Mama was, though. I thought again that she weren't looking for work. She was looking for men and that might as well meant she was looking for trouble. After how things had gone in Barnesville, I didn't really figure that money was going to change her for the better.

Morning time was a pretty busy time, it looked like. Come the middle of the day, Orchard Hill settled down in a little bit and the coming and going pretty much stopped. Me and Little Carl got bored looking out at the empty street. We found a bible that the man had left in the dresser in that room and we occupied ourselves with it a good while. We couldn't read much of it, but there was some colored pictures in it. Little Carl come up with a game of us taking turns telling stories about them pictures. He was pretty good at coming up with things, like I said before.

One of the pictures in that Bible showed a fellow naked except for a piece of white cloth across his lap. He was leaned back on a rock and there was little men with wings—angels, I reckon—up and down a ladder over his head.

Little Carl said that fellow's name was Teddy and he was trying to sleep when them little men with wings come down and got to bothering him, acting like big old drunkard flies buzzing around his eyes and his ears. That made Teddy so mad that he got to chasing them little men and followed them all the way up that ladder. When he got to the top, he had wings, too. Instead of climbing back down, Teddy took to flying and flew back to where he had been sleeping before. When he got down there, Teddy seen that he had growed wings, but he had shrunk and now he weren't no bigger than them little men.

On account of them wings, Teddy couldn't sleep on his back no more. He had to sleep on his stomach and he didn't much care for that.

It wasn't much of a ending, I didn't think. I told Little Carl that it would be better if the story just ended with Teddy having wings and being able to fly. Little Carl said he couldn't end it there on account of that wasn't the end of the story.

It was my turn then and Little Carl picked out a picture of a fellow with a beard holding two big rocks that had writing on them. Folks was standing there, looking at the fellow holding the rocks. The fellow holding the rocks looked right mad about it. I started telling a story about how that fellow had left his rocks setting outside of his house and somebody had come along and wrote on them and he was mad about it.

Little Carl said it would be better if I knowed what they had wrote on the rocks. I tried to make something up, but I weren't able to come up with nothing.

There come a tapping at the door and then it cracked open a little bit and a man said, "Are you decent?"

I said, "No," on account of I didn't understand what he meant.

Jimmy Gordon poked his head in and looked at us. I don't know what he was expecting, but it weren't me and Little Carl judging by the look on his face. He asked me, "Where's your mama?"

"Gone to look for a job."

"Uh-huh, well. You know when she'll be back?"

"Uh-uh."

"I need to talk to her."

I didn't say nothing back.

"You tell her to come talk to me when she gets here. I'll be down in the store."

"All right."

He scooted out and closed the door. It worried me that he wanted to talk to Mama. I didn't have no idea of what he wanted, but I would have bet anything that it weren't nothing good for us.

We went back to the story about the man holding the two big rocks. Little Carl said, "What if that fellow wrote on them rocks and he's trying to get them other folks to read it?"

I liked that idea, but I couldn't keep my mind on the story. I was thinking about what in the world Jimmy Gordon was wanting with Mama.

When she come in, I started to keep it to myself, but I knowed she'd find out and be mad at me. "The fellow that rented us the room," his name didn't come to me right off, "he wants to talk to you, Mama," I told her. "He said he'd be down in the store."

"He say what it was about?"

"Naw," I said. "Just wanted to talk to you, he said."

She acted like she was scared to go down there and I didn't blame her.

"Did you get a job?"

"Huh?"

"You went out to look for a job. Was you able to find one?"

"I found one fellow that might hire me," she said, but she didn't say nothing else about the hiring fellow. "How long ago when that store fellow come up?"

"Not too long," I told her. She didn't say nothing back to that. "You want us to come with you?"

She thought on that.

I said, "He might want to tell you we got to move on and you would need to remind him that you're a widow woman with two younguns."

"That's right, that's right," Mama said. "It might be good if y'all did come with me."

We followed her down them wooden steps to the bottom and Mama knocked on the back door to the store.

Jimmy Gordon snatched that door right open, like he had been standing there waiting on us. "Come in, come in," he said and I didn't like it at all.

There is something about the way folks act when they're about to try and do something bad to you, trying to get you to not worry so that when they hurt you, you don't have a chance to fight back as much. That's the way that man was acting. I reckon it was how I had acted with that little colored boy at the well that day. It's the way a lot of folks acts when they go to sell you something.

We walked in and he motioned Mama to a chair to sit down and she did. Me and Little Carl stood there beside her.

"You boys may want to go out in the store and look around some while me and your mama talk," Jimmy Gordon said to us and then smiled real big. "If you find anything you want to buy, I can give you a discount on it."

I didn't know what discount meant, but I knowed the fellow was trying to get shed of us. "We bought all we need yesterday," I said to him and done my best to look mean. "We can set here just fine."

He give us a look and then said to Mama, "I been thinking about you looking for a job. It ain't right for a woman a widow woman to be trying to find a job so soon after her husband has died." That man didn't know nothing about when Daddy had died nor when this Judge fellow, her made-up husband, had died neither.

"I need to work to feed my younguns," she said.

"A woman like you don't need to work," he said to her. I thought that was a right nice thing for him to her, but she acted like he had said something mean to her. She twisted her mouth up and was about to let him have it, it looked like to me. Right quick the man said, "I mean a woman with some money saved up."

"What you want me to do?"

"It's this store, Mrs. Justice," he said to her. I caught that he had said "Justice" and not "Judge," but I didn't say nothing. I wondered if Mama had caught it, but I don't think she did.

"What about it, Jimmy Gordon?"

"When my daddy died, I sold his farm and bought this place. I weren't never no good at farming so I thought I would try my hand running a store. I done alright the first year or two. The past couple of years have been a good bit tighter, though."

Mama didn't say nothing through this, only looked at this Jimmy Gordon in his eyes like she was trying to see right inside the fellow's head.

He went on about the store and his troubles, "This year has been real tough on me on account of I started carrying clothes for women."

"Why is that a problem for you?"

"I am right ashamed to admit it, but I made a mistake. I don't know enough about women and their clothes to have done it."

I figured then he was going to offer Mama a job. He didn't.

"I done extended myself with the bank to the point they won't loan me no more," Jimmy Gordon said. "Now I'm in the danger of losing all of it."

"Uh-huh."

"Renting this room to you helped me a good bit, but when I went to the bank to pay up, it turned out that I was further behind than I thought I was."

"What do you think I can do to help you out with this?"

"Give me some of that money you got."

Mama looked at him like he had cussed her. "I ain't giving you no money. I'll pay you rent by the month, but..."

The man said, "No, no, no. I ain't saying it right. I don't intend for you to give it to me. I mean for you to loan it to me, just like the bank does."

"I ain't no bank, Jimmy Gordon. I'm just a poor widow woman trying to take care of my two younguns with the money from my husband. I don't believe I need to be getting into the loaning people money business."

The man acted like either Mama just weren't understanding him or that he weren't doing something right to make her understand. His face like to have rolled up on itself looking at Mama and figuring what he needed to say next. I seen pretty clear that he didn't intend on us getting out of that store back-room without Mama making him some kind of promise of the money. I wondered if I was strong enough to knock him out of the way and if I did whether Mama would run out the door or stop and help him up. There weren't no telling.

He said, "I am planning for this to be legal and everything. It won't be no risk for you on account of me owning the store. If I don't pay you back by the end of the year, you get the store. You can't get no better than that."

Mama looked like she liked that idea and I knowed we was sunk. She said, "I reckon a woman might have better luck selling clothes for women."

"That's what I was thinking," he said and kind of smiled and then said right quick, "though I hope it doesn't come to that."

Jimmy Gordon said that he understood that, but that he was in right tight spot with the bank and would need to know something tomorrow on account of them getting after him so bad. Mama said she would think on it that night.

As soon as we got back upstairs, I said, "You can't do that, Mama! We ain't got nothing if you give that man the money."

"We'll get it back or we'll get that store," Mama said. "You seen what nice things he sells and the pretty price he puts on them. His prices is too high or he'd do more business. If I run that place, I bet I could sell everything in there for a cheaper price and then buy up some more things to sell after that."

Mama was intent on it and I knowed I couldn't stop it. That didn't stop me from one last try. "You give him our living money, you going to have to get a job sure enough."

She looked at me, mad that I had said it. "I know that. I was going to get a job no matter what anyhow." I knowed blame well that she weren't. She would have laid up in that store's upstairs room till there weren't a blamed penny of that money left.

"Where?" I asked her. "Where you going to get a job at?"

"With the man that runs that silo. He needs a girl to work in the office, he said. I told him I could do it and he said he would hire me next week."

"Mama, you don't know how to work in no office. You can't hardly read and you don't do good with numbers," I said. "Don't you reckon that fellow is looking at you and thinking of going at it as soon as he gets a chance?"

She slapped me hard enough that it made my teeth hurt. "What I do I do to keep you and your brother from starving to death. You need to show me some respect, boy."

I knowed what I could say wouldn't do no good anyway, but I reckon like all folks headed towards hell, I felt the need to go down squealing. "Be a whore then."

She hit me so hard that I fell and hit my head on the footboard to the bed. "You say anything like that to me again and I promise you" Only she didn't finish it. She looked at me like she could have stuck them scissors in me, though. I knowed the promise.

I didn't say nothing else to her about the money. The next morning I made sure that I got up when she did and got me and Little Carl ready as quick as I could. When she was ready to go, we was standing by the door, waiting to leave so she couldn't very well go without us. She didn't look like she liked it, but Mama took us with her to meet with Jimmy Gordon.

"I'm going to let you have the money," Mama said to him as soon as we come in through the door.

"You're not letting me have it," he told her. "You are loaning it to me against the store. If I don't pay you, you get the store."

"Right," Mama said. "That's what I meant. I just wanted to say that I had thought about the whole thing and I trust you to do right by me on this."

"And I expect the same," he said to her. "I don't want this to be a problem for me, either. If I thought for a second you were the kind of woman that would look for a way to cheat a man, I wouldn't have asked you to loan me this money. There are a lot of folks in this world that you can't trust. I believe I can trust you and I sure hope I'm not making a mistake."

Jimmy Gordon had drawed up papers and he gave them to Mama. She looked at them, but I knowed she couldn't read good enough to know what they said. She signed them with her scratches and handed them back and then she reached in her pocket and pulled out that bag of gold double eagles and handed him the whole bag.

She didn't count them and he didn't neither. "That's all I got," Mama told him. "If you need more, you can't get it from me."

"This will be enough," Jimmy Gordon with all our money told her. "You done a good deed to me, Widow Justice and I want to do one to you. After the store closes tonight, I want you to come with me to the Orchard Hill Café." That was the name of that eating place we had went to before.

Mama smiled but then she looked mad and said, "I am a widow woman with two younguns. I can't up and go off whenever I want to."

"I ain't taking *them* to supper," he said like it was some kind of horse trade he was making. "I'll bring them something they can eat till we get back. How about that?"

I ain't got to tell you that Mama thought that was just fine. She wore her fancy outfit, the red dress, that night while me and Little Carl eat salt fish and crackers and some pears Jimmy Gordon had brought.

"I'll have your mama back before too late," he said to us as they went out the door.

Mama didn't say nothing. She hadn't said much of nothing since we had come back to the room earlier. I reckon she figured that we would eat instead of following her, but to be honest with you I weren't much worried no more. She had done give away the money as far as I was concerned. Now I just wondered what stupid thing she would do next that would get us put out with nothing left at all.

Me and Little Carl eat our fill and then tried to tell more stories about them Bible pictures, but weren't neither one of us interested in that. There weren't no whole lot else to do in that room except sleep. I wished we had got a pack of cards from Uncle Henry before we left Barnesville, but you can't never fix things after they're done.

The food Jimmy Gordon had brought us was pretty good and I eat as much as I could. A full belly made it easier to sleep and I wanted to go to sleep before Mama got home so I wouldn't have to look at her.

Little Carl didn't eat much and acted like he weren't interested in going to sleep neither. We tried to look out the window at the folks on the street, but there weren't none. About that time, Little Carl had one of his idiot spells, but it was worse than he usually had. He fell in the floor and when I tried to get him up, he jerked away from me. I tried to pull him up onto the bed, but I couldn't. He had done got too big for me to do that. I wound up just setting on the floor with him.

I dozed off. I don't know how long we was there, setting in the floor. Finally Mama come home. I heard her clomping up the steps and heard her laugh. I was afraid the man might be coming back with her, that they might be planning to go at it here with me and Little Carl setting in the room with them or that she might tell us to go outside.

I listened and didn't hear nobody but her, though. She throwed the door open and near about fell on top of us where we was setting. "Mama, Little Carl's having a bad one," I told her. "I ain't never seen him have one like this."

Mama looked at him and kind of grinned. "My little idiot." Then she looked at me. "You're just like your daddy," she said. "You always bring trouble." I knowed the smell I smelled was liquor.

She walked around us and laid face down on the bed. I got up from Little Carl and looked at her. She was already asleep. I pulled her shoes off of her and she didn't wake up.

"Mama brought the devil home."

I looked around and Little Carl was sitting up, looking at me.

"Mama brought the devil home," he said again.

I wanted to hit him, but I wanted to run, too. I didn't do neither one. I done what I needed to do. I got him up out of the floor and onto the bed. He was asleep in a little bit.

I was mad. I don't reckon I had no right to be. Mama was a grown woman and she could do what she wanted to do. She was taking care of the two of us, too, in her own way. I was just having a hard time thinking that it was the best thing for us, what she had come up with.

Then I got to thinking about Gladys. There she had give us a whole lot more money than we was expecting even though her and Mama weren't getting along. I wondered if Mr. Caudell had beat her bad when he seen that money gone, but I knowed he probably had. Here she had been took in by this fellow and treated nice, it looked to me. I didn't see why she had turned around and give away his money like she had.

Mama was snoring loud and I wondered how in the world Little Carl was able to sleep through it. I laid down myself for a minute, thinking that if they could sleep, maybe I could too, but I couldn't. I couldn't quit thinking about Mama giving away the money and wondering what in the world we was going to do now.

Finally I got up and looked out that window. I looked back at Mama and Little Carl and figured they would likely sleep through the night without waking up and causing me no more trouble. Maybe if I walked a while, I'd be able to sleep when I got back.

It was a dark night and so quiet you wouldn't think there was a soul alive in Orchard Hill and maybe not in the world. It had been clouding up late in the day so whatever moon there was was behind the clouds. I went down the back steps and around to the main street and took to walking toward the middle of town.

Nothing good had ever happened for us, I didn't reckon. Mama had done give our money to that man. If he paid us back, it would be a little bit every now and then. We would wind up spending it on Mama's foolishness. I didn't want him to give us the store, neither, though because I knowed we didn't know nothing about running it.

I come to the Methodist Church towards the end of the street and seen a dog come out from behind the building. It was a skinny dark-colored dog that made me wonder whether it belonged to anybody or was a stray that eat out of garbage piles. I knelt down and whistled and it come to me. I rubbed its head and it licked me. I wished I had brought something with me to feed it but I didn't have nothing. Even though all I could do was rub its head, the little dog was happy to be with me. I couldn't feed it, I couldn't do nothing for it, but it acted like it liked me. That made me feel good.

I felt a little rain coming down and I kind of wondered what was going to happen to that little dog now. I thought about picking him up and taking him back to our room with me. I didn't know whether he would let me pick him up or not, though. Sometimes a dog will snap at you if you go to do something it ain't ready for.

Just then the dog raised its head up and down like it smelled something good and then he barked. I smelled it too. I looked back and that's when I seen it. The store was burning.

I took off running.

When I got around to the back, I seen the stairs was burnt away like they had been burning a long time. I hollered up there, hoping I could wake Mama and Little Carl. I run around to the front and the fire had busted the front window out. I jumped through the window and run through the fire to try to get to them inside stairs.

The door to the stairs was locked. The smoke was so thick I couldn't hardly see. I looked around and seen a metal door stop that was shaped like a little boat. I picked it up and beat it against the doorknob till it broke off. The door still didn't open and I had to stick the skinny edge of the door stop into the gap between the door and the jamb and pry it open.

The fire hadn't got to the inside stairs until I opened that door. Everything smelled like kerosene and I couldn't hardly breathe. When I opened the door, it sucked fire and I was sure it had set my back on fire, but I didn't stop. I went running up the steps and when I got to the top, I throwed the door open and run into the room where Mama and Little Carl was asleep.

I shook Mama and tried to wake her up. I grabbed Little Carl's arm and pulled him back to the stairs and pushed him ahead of me. We got to the bottom and the fire had caught on the last few inside stair steps. I got Little Carl outside and pushed him into the street and then went back up for Mama.

Mama was still sound asleep laying right where she had flopped down on that bed. I pulled her and shook her and hollered, but the smoke was so thick up there by then that I knowed I couldn't stay there for long. I pulled her out of the bed and dragged her to the stairs. I tried to get her to stand up, but she was still too drunk I reckon. We made it a few steps down, maybe half the way, before we fell and tumbled one over the other to the bottom.

We hit the steps that were burned and went through them. I had to pull Mama up but when I did, my leg wouldn't hold me up and I knowed there weren't no way I could walk it. So I crawled, pulling Mama along with me until we was outside and I could catch my breath. My chest and my throat still hurt and my eyes was still watering from the smoke and that kerosene smell but at least we was alive.

The building was burning good by then. I looked over at Little Carl. He was sitting up in the middle of the street. "Mama brought the devil home," he said. And I knowed for sure he was speaking the truth.

Mama laughed when he said it. I looked around at her and seen that she was propped up on her elbows looking at the fire with the rest of us. She had throwed up on the front of her fancy red dress and mess was all over her chin and down her front. I was hoping that she had got the whiskey out of her because I figured I was going to need her help on account of my leg.

I wanted to move, to get us up and away from there, but I couldn't do it. My legs was out in front of me. The right one was bent at the knee. The left one was bent at the knee and then below it was bent again and was starting to hurt. I could feel a throbbing that made the hurting come and go and it felt like it was going to get worse before it got better.

Little Carl's head was all leaned back with his mouth hung open. He had slipped into one of his idiot spells.

Chapter VI
REFORM

❧⊰⊱❧

There we was sitting in the middle of the street when I heard somebody and looked around to see two fellows trotting our way. One of them was a tall skinny man and the other one was tall but not as skinny. The first man had a gun. "Anybody still in there?"

Before I could answer the other one said, "Good Lord has saved Orchard Hill with his cleansing rain."

It lightninged a ways off and there was a roll of thunder that sounded like it was coming slow across the sky. "I don't reckon," I told him. "Weren't nobody living there but the three of us."

The rain got a little harder and the second fellow said, "How did it start?"

The first one didn't wait on us to answer. He said to the second, "Get over to the Methodist Church and start ringing that bell. It quits raining, we going to have trouble."

"The Good Lord," the second fellow started to say before the first man cut him off.

"God damn it, James, get over to the church and ring that bell." This time the second fellow took off.

"I think my leg is broke," I told the man, but he weren't paying me no attention. I know he had to think he had run up on a whole family of idiots, setting there watching the fire burn in the rain.

He crossed the street to a house and beat on the door till a fat man wearing long johns answered the door. I could see them talking. The fat man went back in and the skinny fellow with the gun come back over to us.

"Butler's letting us use his front room until the storm is over. Come on."

"My leg is broke," I said again.

"Uh-huh. How about this one?" he asked, pointing to Mama.

"Just drunk, I think."

"And the boy?"

"He ain't right," I told him.

"Damned if y'all ain't a sight," the fellow said to me. "A flat out sight."

About that time, the church bells started ringing.

The man with the gun was a skinny man, but he was sure a lot stronger than he looked. He picked me up and toted me over to the Butler house like I weren't nothing. He started to lay me on the fat man's sofa, but the man said, "No! On the floor! On the floor!" So he put me down on a little rug that was laid in front of the fireplace.

In a minute he come back toting Little Carl. Little Carl was putting up a fight. I figured it was because he didn't want to be separated from Mama. The skinny man set him in the floor next to me and said, "Stay here with your—Y'all are brothers, ain't you?"

"Yes, sir."

"Set here with your brother while I go get that woman."

Little Carl was getting up before the tall man could straighten hisself.

"Stay here, boy."

Little Carl kicked at the tall man and the tall man swatted him with the back of his hand.

"I don't care if you a moron or not, boy, you kick me and I'm going to plant a foot up your ass that you won't forget for a while."

Little Carl quit kicking, but still made to go toward the door.

The fat man come over and grabbed ahold of Little Carl. "I've got him."

"Thank you, Butler."

The tall man went out the door and the fat man said, "What in the hell happened over there?"

"I don't rightly know," I told him. "Mama come home drunk. I got her and Little Carl — my brother here — in the bed. I walked down the street and seen a dog and the next thing I knowed the building was burning."

The fat man made a face like he wanted to spit. "Damned lucky it rained. The whole town would have burned if this had happened on a dry night."

I didn't feel too lucky. That throbbing in my leg was starting to make it hard for me to think about anything else. I must have been looking like I felt. "I think my leg is broke."

"We ain't got a doctor around here right now," he told me. "You going to have to wait till Beaton gets you over to Griffin."

I nodded. I hadn't never been to a doctor and weren't in no hurry to go to one, but that throbbing leg was about to kill me.

The tall skinny fellow, Beaton I guessed his name was now, come back in. "I seen her headed towards the store. You sure there weren't nobody else in there?"

"No, sir," I told him. "Weren't nobody but me and him and her."

"Well, now there ain't nobody but you and him, son. She run inside and then the porch caved in and I didn't see nothing else of her."

"She might have gone out the back way," I said.

The man shook his head. "Might have, son, but I don't think so. I hate it for you, but I think your Mama got burned up."

People started coming to the door then and Beaton started telling them what to do. They was working to be sure that the fire didn't set the next building on fire and so they went to get a bucket line going over there. My leg was hurting so bad I wasn't paying much mind to them. Some more folks come in and walked right by Beaton without saying nothing. One was a old woman that come over to me and got down on the floor next to me. She pulled up my britches leg and when she did, it liked to have killed me. I thought I was going to throw up it hurt so bad.

"Looks clean," she hollered. There was a old man with her. She told him something then, but I couldn't pay much attention. She looked over at Butler. "You got whiskey?"

Butler didn't much like telling her that he did. You could see it in his face. He went out of the room though and come right back with a bottle of branded liquor and a little mug.

The old woman took it and poured some whiskey in the mug and told me to drink it. I shook my head. "I can't drink liquor."

"Drink it."

I swallowed it down. It burned my throat and I thought again I might throw up. About the time I got it down to stay, she had done poured me another one and made me drink it. She poured me a third one, but there just weren't no way I could drink it right then. I laid back and felt that liquor warm me up. In a few minutes, that leg throbbing didn't hurt so bad, though I could still feel my heart beating through it.

My first sample of bonded liquor put me out of my right mind a little bit. I wondered if that was how Little Carl felt when he had a idiot spell. It didn't hurt, but it made me feel like I couldn't be sure about what was going on. I didn't like it at the time. But like most men, I got better at drinking liquor later on.

That old woman had been a nurse, she said. Her husband said she was right good at it and had done a little bit of doctoring on their own younguns over the years. I thought she done pretty good though I didn't have nothing to compare her to. "You numb yet?" she asked me. "Can you still feel that leg throbbing?"

I tried to tell her that I could feel it, but that it weren't as bad as before. I couldn't talk just right on account of the liquor. She seemed to understand what I was saying though because she started telling her husband what to do to help me.

I remember the coming and going of folks through the night. The fire was still burning, but the rain had saved the other buildings, they said. About the time one of them would thank Jesus for his saving grace, another one would cuss the fact that the whole thing happened in the first place.

The old woman set there with me. She got to looking at my leg and then her husband pulled real hard on it two times. They cut my britches' leg off and then they wrapped my leg up. Somebody toted me to that sofa Butler didn't want me on. I slept off and on.

When I woke up, I had to go pee something awful and the old man toted me to another room and got me a slop jar. My stomach felt like I had swallowed rocks and they were all trying to get out. The last thing I remember about being in Butler's house was throwing up on his little rug.

Little Carl was setting next to me when I woke up the next time.

"Little Carl? Where are we?"

"We in Griffin."

"How did we get to Griffin?"

"A deputy brought us," Little Carl told me.

I looked around and seen that we was in jail. There was three fellows in the next cell sound asleep, all three of them snoring to beat the band. My leg hurt, but nothing like how it had hurt before.

"He brought us here this morning. I kept hoping you would wake up. He rode us by a cotton mill here that just opened and it had a smokestack that was blowing clouds up in the air to where you couldn't hardly see the sunshine."

"How about that," I said, wishing I had seen it. "Why did he put us in here?"

"They think we killed Caudell."

"Caudell?"

"Uh-huh. Gladys said Mama killed him, but since they didn't find Mama, they keeping us."

I made myself set up. We was on a straw mattress that was laying on top of a metal frame. Them fellows was sleeping mighty good on it and I reckoned that I had been, too, though it was a might hard for just setting.

My left leg was in a splint, tied and doctored and looking like it would do for walking if need be. I started to get up. When I did, I lost my balance and went down in a swirl. That wooden splint bumped against the bars and made a big racket. Them fellows in the next cell woke up and hollered for me to quiet down but then they was right back to snoring. Little Carl grabbed me and got me back up on the bunk.

"You ain't going to be able to walk for a while," he told me. "They said your leg was broke, but it weren't too bad."

In a little bit, a man come in with trays of food that he slid through for us. It was pretty good, but I reckon I was pretty hungry by that time. He fed me and Little Carl, but he let them fellows sleep. They started waking up a while later, hollering about being hungry, but the man didn't pay them no attention and they went back to sleep.

We was in there for near on a week before Judge Miller come to Griffin to hear cases. They took me and Little Carl together to the courthouse. Since I was in a splint, they didn't worry about me running, I don't guess, but they put a chain around Little Carl's leg and made him walk dragging it till he got to where he could set down.

The judge said a bunch of legal things and then another man talked. Beaton come in and told about the fire and finding us in the street and seeing our mama and then losing her. The judge didn't much like that losing-her part and he asked Beaton a lot of questions about it and Beaton finally said she had probably died in the fire.

The judge said there weren't no proof of that, that they hadn't found no body. Beaton said, "Judge, I don't mean to be disrespectful. I been to a few fires and they don't always leave proof of what got burned up. I seen a house fire out at Brooks that killed six folks but we didn't find bones but for two of them on account of the fire burning so hot."

The judge said something about the house fire in Brooks involving a still, but Beaton stuck with his story. Finally, the judge told him to get down from that chair and to quit talking.

A man name of Barney Grant got up and talked then. It turned out that he had owned the building where the store and our room was. Jimmy Gordon didn't own it at all. He only worked for this Grant fellow, running the store. Hadn't nobody seen him since before the fire.

Grant was mad about his building. He said me and Little Carl ought to have to spend the rest of our lives in jail on account of it, but the judge, he didn't much think so and the two of them argued about it.

Finally somebody asked me how old I was. I didn't rightly know. I knowed Gladys was fifteen because Mama had said so one time, but that had been a year ago. I figured I was right behind her so I told the judge that I thought I was near about fifteen.

Had I been baptized? I didn't know for sure what that meant, though I knowed it had something to do with church. "No, sir," I told him. That set him and the rest of them to talking.

I didn't understand and can't remember all that the judge said then. When he beat on the desk, he said me and Little Carl weren't guilty. I understood that much of it. Then he said he was sending us to Pike County.

I thought that they had meant to let us go. They didn't. It turned out that we was not guilty in one place but another place wanted to have a chance at us.

When the judge said we weren't guilty, that set well with some in the room and not so well with the rest, especially Grant. Another fellow come and took me and Little Carl and put us in the back of a car and hauled us to the jail in Zebulon.

It was the first time we had ever rode in a automobile. I don't know what make it was now, but I remember it made so much noise that we couldn't hardly hear each other talk in the back seat. We had walked most everywhere we went. Riding a mule or riding in a wagon was a good bit faster than walking. Riding in a car made us both think we was having some kind of dream where you fly except this weren't no dream and we were together in it anyhow. The trip from Griffin to Zebulon didn't take no time. The only time we stopped was when we crossed the railroad tracks at one place. There was a train headed to Macon that had stopped to switch out cars.

The fellow driving us to Zebulon asked us if we was hungry and we said we was. He reached into a paper sack he had with him and brought out some pieces of cake that was wrapped up in newspaper.

He handed them back to us. Little Carl said, "Thank you," and the man shook his head. We ate the cake while the train went by. When it was finally past us, we eased on across the tracks and before long, we come to Zebulon.

When we got to the jail in Zebulon, the driver toted me inside while Little Carl walked beside us, dragging them chains on his legs. Me and Little Carl got put in different cells, but we was next to each other so it weren't too bad. There weren't nobody else in this jail, which is good because there weren't but them two cells.

I ain't going to go on about the time we was there. We didn't have no window we could see out. They had a bible they let us look at, but it didn't have no pictures in it. Little Carl was having his spells more and didn't get to doing them stories about the rabbits that wore clothes and talked so all in all, it was a rough time. It went on like that for near about two weeks.

Me and Little Carl set in the jail a while longer. When they finally took us to court, I was out of the splint, but still hobbling. They let me use a crutch to get to the seat they had for me. The judge let Mr. Howard talk and he let the fellow they called "the state" talk.

Didn't nobody know nothing about Daddy, it didn't sound like. If they did they didn't let on. I was scared they might have found him when they was looking for that colored boy, but they hadn't. It was Mr. Caudell they talked about. He was dead and they thought Mama had killed him.

When they was done, the judge said he wanted to think about what had been said.

Me and Little Carl got took back to jail while the judge thought about it and he done a lot of thinking. We set in that jail three more days before some fellows come and got Little Carl. They was going to take him to the hospital at Milledgeville because that was what the judge had said to do.

I will tell you that the next three days, the time I spent in that little cell all by myself all day long was the worst days of my life. I seen then why folks hated jail so much. It weren't bad when you had somebody to keep you company. By yourself, though, it was about the worst place in the world.

They took me back to the courthouse finally and had the judge talk to me.

"Son, the court has ruled that your mama died in the fire in Orchard Hill on the sixteenth of last month. We have ruled that your brother is a moron and not responsible for his actions. He has been placed in the state hospital in Milledgeville.

"You're too little to be sent to prison. There's a new place down close to Milledgeville called the Boys' Reformatory. You are going to be put there for the next five years."

"You ain't going to hang me?"

"No, son," the judge said. He didn't say it kindly nor meanly. He said it to me like I was a idiot that didn't understand what had just been said. I reckon he was right.

"Is Gladys all right?"

"Your sister is going to be fine, I think. She specifically asked not to be here today. It was her testimony that your mother killed her husband."

"Her husband? Gladys weren't married to Mr. Caudell."

The judge looked down at me. "Your sister and Mr. Caudell were married two months ago, according to the paperwork she showed us."

That sure didn't make no sense. I said, "No, sir. Mr. Caudell was married already."

"Mr. Caudell's previous relationship was of the common-law variety. Your sister had papers filed at the courthouse. The Reverend Peter Tate signed the marriage license. He said he had the ceremony at his church one afternoon when it was raining too much for Caudell to do any plowing."

I shook my head, not believing what the judge said, though I knowed he didn't have no reason to lie to me.

"Your sister had the documents, son," the judge said. "She was very unhappy that we did not recover the money your mother stole."

"She give it to Jimmy Gordon or whatever his name was."

"There was no 'Jimmy Gordon,'" the judge told me. "The man who was running that store didn't own it. He didn't own much of anything. We haven't been able to find him, and I don't believe we will."

Sure enough, I got sent to Milledgeville, only not to the crazy house like Little Carl was. The deputies handcuffed me to a rail in a car where they kept suitcases. It weren't bad though the fellow that run the train acted like he thought it was.

The reformatory was right nice. A man and his wife run it and there was near about two hundred boys there. In the morning we eat and done schooling. Then we worked on the farm they had and then we eat again and then we went to bed.

Mr. Felton was the man that was my teacher. He was a good-sized fellow, but I figure a couple of the boys could have got together and whipped him without much trouble. He didn't never act scared, though. He done our lessons for us and we learned. I learned how to do my numbers pretty good and done right good with reading and done a little bit with writing.

It was supposed to be rough on us, I reckon, but it weren't. There weren't a boy I knowed there what had got as much to eat where he had come from. Some of them missed their mamas and some missed their daddies, but none of them missed how they had been before they got there.

Me and three more boys stayed in one room. It weren't bad at all. All three of them other ones could take care of theirselves so I didn't have to dress them or put them to bed or nothing. I got regular sleep and good food and that near about made up for the schooling. Even that, like I said, weren't too bad.

Mr. Felton talked the man that run the picture show in Milledgeville into letting us come and see the show there one time a month. You didn't get to go unless you was good and done all your school work.

I reckon it was the picture show that got me interested in reading and writing even more than Little Carl and them talking rabbits had done.

My leg healed about as good as it could. It weren't never right and I hobbled on it a little bit. When the weather turned, it would throb and hurt. I got to where I could tell when rain was coming.

In all that time, I never heard nothing from Little Carl nor from Gladys. I sure didn't hear nothing from Mama. I still didn't believe she had died in the fire. I just didn't believe it.

We had visiting days once every month, but I didn't have nobody visit me. That didn't bother me none because I weren't expecting nobody. It was the boys that had folks to come but them folks didn't come, them was the boys that I felt bad for.

Most of the boys there would come for a year or two or maybe three and then be gone. You would get to know one and turn around and he was gone. I stayed a long time, longer than anybody else I knowed about.

Along about my last year there, a new man name of Harrison got hired on. He was supposed to just watch the boys at night, listen out for anybody that might be up with a belly ache or for fellows fighting after the lights was turned out. Harrison liked to come into the rooms with the new littler boys, though, and I heard tell some bad stories about what he done when he went in there.

Somebody told on Harrison to the head man. Harrison got the idea that it was me that told on him, but it weren't. He caught me by myself a day or two after that and pushed me up against the wall and shut the door. He told me to do something that I didn't want to do and I told him I wouldn't.

"White trash, you going to do what I tell you to do and if you say anything to the boss about it, I'll hurt you so bad that crippled leg of yours will be the best thing left."

Harrison was taller than me, but by then I had filled out a good bit. I didn't know whether I could take him or not, but I knowed I would be able to put up a fight. I didn't say nothing back to him. I looked him over and started thinking how I could knock him down and get out of there.

"Get on your knees."

I went like I was bending over and I run at him and hit him in the belly with my head as hard as I could. He hit back against the door and went down. I put my knee between his legs and then started hitting him in the face and then I got up and stumbled, but I got the door open.

I don't know where I would have run to, but it didn't matter. The head man was coming down the hall with one of the fellows that had been there a long time. I near about run into them. Harrison come out the door, hollering, "You little son of a bitch," but he shut up when he seen them other two.

They fired Harrison and I admit I was glad they did.

When I got called to the head man's office a day or two after that, I figured I was in trouble, but I weren't. The head man said it was coming up on time for me to be released. I didn't say nothing back because I don't reckon I had thought on it none.

"You have one more year, but we're going to let you serve that on probation. You stay out of trouble and you'll turn 21 a free man."

I must have looked as foolish as I felt. I didn't know what I was going to do if the Reformatory turned me out.

The head man said, "You'll be able to live with your sister when you leave here."

I said, "I wish I could, but my sister don't want to have nothing to do with me, I don't believe."

"Might not have at one time, but she's done got beyond that now," the head man said to me. "She sent a letter to the judge about it nigh on a year ago."

I didn't know what to say back to that. It worried me, wondering what Gladys might be thinking to do now. I near about didn't want to go, but I was getting to be a young man, like the head fellow had said. I needed to be out.

The head man had Mr. Felton work with me on some things I would need to do when I got out. One of the things he give me that I thought was real nice was a little pack of paper and some envelopes and some stamps and a good pencil. He told me he wanted me to use it to write to him and let him know how I was doing.

I got let out a day or two after that. Between walking and catching rides, it took me two more days to get to the Caudell place. I give that paper and things to a man in a car that said he was driving to Florida. At the time, I hadn't never heard tell of Florida so it didn't mean nothing to me. He said he would send me a letter from Florida if I wanted him to, but I told him that was alright.

The last ride I caught took me a couple of miles away so I didn't have far to walk. When I come walking up to the house, I seen my sister out in the yard with a youngun. I thought at first it was the baby, but I seen right quick that it weren't. It was a boy and a good-sized one at that.

"Hey!" I hollered. They both looked up at about the same time. He was a cute little fellow and to tell you the truth, he put me in mind of Little Carl right then, only a wider and stronger version of him.

"Herman, this is your uncle," she told the little boy when I come walking up to their house. The little fellow looked at me and I looked at him but didn't neither one of us say nothing.

Gladys looked a good bit like Mama, but she had more meat on her than Mama ever had. I asked her, "Why did you get me out?"

She looked away from me and said, "I reckon I felt bad about putting you in."

"You didn't put me in."

"I did," she said. "Come on." She went in the house and I followed her, toting the sack they had give me when I left the reformatory. The house wasn't as nice as it had been, I don't reckon, since there weren't nobody around to work on it. The front room ceiling had a big brown spot where the roof leaked. Some of Caudell's pretties had got broke and was setting here and there like they was waiting to be fixed though that weren't going to happen.

"How you getting by?" I asked her. "You farming?"

"I got some colored hands living down in our old place. They raise a right smart of cotton and price has been good."

"Who is Herman's daddy?" I asked her. "Caudell?"

"That don't matter."

I didn't reckon that it did, but I wondered anyhow.

She didn't ask me about the reformatory and she didn't say nothing about Little Carl. I didn't ask her nothing else. I figured I would find out what I needed to know when I needed to know it.

"Did Mama really give that money to some man?"

"Uh-huh."

Gladys shook her head. "I swear that woman is about as foolish as they come. I thought y'all was going to Newnan and then she winds up in Orchard Hill. I reckon I was right foolish myself giving her that money."

I didn't say nothing back to that.

She put me up in the bedroom across from where her and the youngun slept. When I got up that first morning, the colored fellow name of Blink was already there at the back door, getting money from her for fertilizer.

"I don't let them run no account up on me," she told me. "I give him two dollars and he might run off with my two dollars. I let him run up a bill at Stricklands' and either one of them might lie and rob me of a lot more than two dollars."

That sounded like a right smart way to do business, I thought. It was sure smarter than what Daddy would have ever done if he had ever got to where he could do it. I asked her, "What you want me to do?"

"I ain't got that figured out," she said. "I can let you use the mule to go to town if you want to get you a job there. If you want to sharecrop, Pete Tate and his boy need somebody." She didn't offer to let me take over from the hands she had working our old place. That was fine by me because I didn't know that it would be a good idea for us to do worry over money together.

I spent the first few days working on her house. I say it was her house because she had legal title to it. I didn't understand how in the world she had done it, but she had. I got up there and fixed the only bad spot I could find on the roof and was put in mind of Judge the Roofer.

Little Herman was a funny little fellow. I slipped up and called him Little Carl a couple of times. He didn't have no bad spot on his head, though, and he talked right plain even though he was still so little. The little fellow didn't act like Gladys was his mama. He acted like he worked for her, doing what little he could. Like I said, it was right funny.

I went to town after I had been there a few days. The place hadn't changed much except for the cars. Where before there hadn't been nothing but mules and wagons and a few horses, now there was a good many cars, too.

I asked the man at the general store if he knowed anybody needed somebody to work for them.

"What you know how to do?"

I said, "I done some farming, mostly. I was in the reformatory the last few years."

"How old a man are you?"

"I'm about twenty, I reckon."

"You look like you favor that left leg when you walk."

"I do. It got broke when I was a youngun and it never did set right."

"You know how to work a pump?"

"I pumped a well before."

"A gasoline pump. You ever work one of them?"

"No, but I reckon I can learn how to do it."

He took me around to the back of his store. There was a red pump back there with a glass tank up on top of it. He showed me how to pump the handle while I kept a eye on that tank. It was marked to show how many gallons there was. I would pump the gas up in there, pull the release and let it go into the tank of the car and then give a slip of paper to the fellow running the cash register inside, showing how many gallons I had pumped.

It weren't hard work and I told the fellow I thought I could do it. I saved as much money as I could from my pay every week. Herman got sick twice and I wound up spending part of the money I had saved getting medicine for him. I knowed Gladys had some more money, but she acted like she didn't and I wound up paying.

Herman was a sight, though. I reckon I loved the little fellow more than anybody except Little Carl. I told him that if he was extra good, he could go with me on a trip to Milledgeville in September.

§

September finally came and I had done cleared it with the man that run the store to be off on a Monday. I knew if I left Saturday night, I could be in Milledgeville to see Little Carl Sunday afternoon and be back to work on Tuesday.

It was a worser trip than I had expected it to be. There was a drizzling rain when we closed the store on Saturday and Gladys said Herman needed to stay home. I took the mule and rode as far as I could, spent the night in a shed on the road outside of Thomaston and got up the next day to ride the rest of the way. I got there later than I thought I would. There was a whole lot of folks there on account of it being Sunday.

It weren't hard to figure out where to go. I just went to where most of the folks was going. A woman with a nurse outfit on was setting at the desk, telling folks where they would find their kinfolks. I waited till my turn and went up. I told her who I was there to see.

She went through a bunch of papers and said, "I don't believe we have anyone by that name."

"Could you look again? I know they brought him down here after the trial."

She looked like she had swallowed a pickle. She opened up a drawer in her desk and pulled out another paper and looked at it. "Your brother is in the criminal ward."

"I want to see him," I told her. "I ain't seen him in seven years, I think."

"It says here that he killed a man," she said, "although it might have been a woman. He's not allowed to see anybody."

"Little Carl didn't kill nobody," I told her. "I killed a little nigger boy, but I didn't do no time for that. They locked me up on account of not finding some money that got stole."

The nurse said, "Sir, your brother is in the criminal ward. There is no visitation in the criminal ward."

I believe that was the maddest I ever been in my life. "I come all the way from Pike County to see him."

"Well, you can't."

When I was in the reformatory, I had learned some things about rules. The more people there are involved in a thing, looks like the more rules they come up with and there is two ways to get around them. You can either fight your way through the rules, but that don't work for long. Or you can buy your way through them. That happens a good bit.

I rode the mule back home.

Around the time I went to Milledgeville, Gladys started getting visits from Jefferson McAlexander, a fellow nearly fifty years old at the time. Jefferson was the kind of fellow that had money but never did spend none of it. Him and Daddy wouldn't have much got along, I don't reckon.

Jeff, as we called him, had been widowed twice but he didn't have no children. He had been in the Army and loved to talk about it. He had been in the Arizona Territory at some point, too, and had killed a Indian while he was there. He carried that Indian's dried-up ear in his pocket for good luck. It seemed to be pretty lucky for him so I didn't discount it.

Gladys had put on a few pounds since Herman was born. She looked like she was about to have another one, but it weren't nothing but fat. Her and Jeff went at it a good bit, but they didn't do it till they thought me and Herman was asleep. To be a old fellow, Jeff sure liked to go at it. Or maybe it was Gladys that liked it. I don't reckon I know really.

Working at the gas pump wasn't paying a lot, but I was learning how to fix cars as long as the problem was a easy one. Folks with cars didn't much want to fix them, they wanted somebody else to do it. I got good at hemming and hawing over a easy problem and asking a high price and then fixing it right quick after the fellow what owned the car left it with me. Folks got to where they would come looking for me when they needed to have their cars worked on.

§

It took a good while to save up the money I needed, but when I did, I borrowed a car and drove back down to Milledgeville. I rode up to the back side of the place, where the folks that worked there come and went. It cost me six silver dollars to get to where I wanted to go.

I had wore a nice suit of clothes and slicked my hair good with grease to where I looked suitable.

The fellow that opened the back door said, "Anybody asks you, you tell them you're his lawyer."

"Uh-huh," I said.

The man unlocked the door and I went in. There was probably thirty or forty folks in there. He took me over to where two fellows was standing, a big one and a little one. "Here he is," the man said.

I looked at the two fellows. The big one was taller than I was. The little one was funny looking. It weren't Little Carl, I didn't think.

I said, "Little Carl?"

The little fellow said, "Are you my daddy?"

When he talked, I knowed it weren't Little Carl. It didn't sound nothing like him. Nothing at all. I turned around to the man I had come in with. "This ain't him."

"Yeah, it is."

I felt like popping him in the mouth, but I didn't. If I had of done that, they would have probably locked me up again.

I left out of there and seen some folks standing over to the side of the place, looking at the ground. I went over there and looked and seen some little markers made out of cast iron. One of the fellows looking said, "It's a shame there is no one here for some of them."

I looked at them little markers and figured out that this was where they was burying the ones that died while they was here. I looked at the graves and then I looked back at the building and I hoped Little Carl was in the grave.

One night, setting at Caudell's with Gladys, I started to telling her what had happened with Little Carl.

"He's where he needs to be," she said. I still don't feel too good about it, but I reckon she was right.

§

Jeff and Gladys got married the next spring. They didn't have no church wedding, what with him being old enough to be her daddy and her already having a youngun. They just went to the courthouse and had the justice of the peace there do it. Jeff moved into the house with us and before long, it was time for me to move out.

The man I worked for at the store pumping gasoline had a spare room in his house and he let me rent it from him for near about nothing. I eat at night with him and his family. They reminded me a good bit of Aunt Clara and Uncle Henry. They didn't have no younguns, but her sister Phoebe lived with them.

His wife was a pretty woman, but Phoebe weren't. She always had a look on her face like she was mad about something. The first time you met her, you thought she was going to come at you, but she weren't. It was just how her face looked.

It was a set-up from the day that man told me that he had a room for rent. First thing I knowed, me and Phoebe got seated next to each other at dinner, got left alone together a good bit and I got invited to family dinners at their grandma's house.

By this time, I had gone at it with some whores. The day I come back from Milledgeville, I took one. I didn't make a show of it like some fellows do. I just done it when I needed to do it.

Phoebe weren't no whore, but like all women, she could have her whorish ways when it suited her. The first time we went at it was when we had got left alone at the house and she told me to come to her room and see if I could help her move some furniture around. It weren't but a few minutes and we was in the bed together.

When she come up telling me that we was going to have a baby, I told Phoebe I didn't want to have no baby while we was living with her folks, so she thought we was going to get married and move out to our own house. I had bought my own car by then and I told her I wanted her to meet my sister, Gladys, and she said she thought she would like to.

When we got to the Caudell place, there was a woman setting on the steps watching Herman hoop-and-sticking around the yard, but it weren't Gladys. We parked the car and went walking up towards the house. When we got closer I knowed just exactly who it was.

"Mama," I said. It was not a question.

"Hey, boy," Mama said. She looked up at me and I seen one of her eyes had been poked out. The lid was open about halfway on that side and you could see things move in there when she would look here and there, but she didn't do nothing to hide it.

"What happened to your eye?"

"A nigger poked it out."

"Nigger man?"

"Uh-huh."

I didn't want to know no more. "This is Phoebe, Mama."

"Hey, Phoebe."

"Hey."

"Gladys and Jeff here?"

"They gone. I'm keeping Herman till they get back."

"When they going to be home?"

"I ain't sure."

"Uh-huh."

Phoebe started acting funny on account of Mama and that poked-out eye and the way Mama would have to turn her head odd to look at you. "We can come back another time."

"We here now," I told her.

"But I wanted to meet Gladys…"

"Come on," I told her and went inside. The kitchen cabinets was about empty and the ice box looked plumb dry. We went through the house, me poking into every room.

Phoebe finally opened her mouth. "What you looking for?"

"Nothing," I said.

"Well, you found it."

"Yeah," I said, "I did." And then I swung.

It was the first time I had hit her even though we had been going together for close to a year by then. I slapped her again, hard enough to knock her into the floor.

She got up crying and I done what I had intended to do later. I kicked her about as hard as I could right in the belly. She hollered and I kicked her again. She curled up in a ball so I went around and kicked her good in the butt. She kept on hollering.

I went outside then and set down next to Mama. "You know where Little Carl is?"

"Dead, ain't he?"

"Uh-huh." It was the last thing I said.

I took Phoebe back to the house. My time with her and with pumping gas was over.

Early the next morning I put my things in a box and toted them to the car and then I eased back down the road to Caudell's. I didn't see Mama nor Herman in the yard. I figured they was inside, eating whatever little bit was left.

I stopped the car in front of the little house where we had all lived and thought about Daddy and the wagon and the day we'd all rode into town to watch the hanging. Then I thought about Little Carl.

Maybe we was the idiots instead of him. One thing was for sure. He'd been right all along about the devil.

I drove on.

THE END

Acknowledgments

I must thank my lovely wife Beth for her support and encouragement. She and Tom Allison, my father-in-law, read the book in its early form and gave me good feedback. Thanks in particular go to my editor Vally Sharpe, whose suggestions improved the work immensely.